SCREAM
BLACK
MURDER

A WorldKrime Mystery

by
Philip McLaren

INTRIGUE
PRESS

Philadelphia

ISBN 1-890768-42-1

Originally published in Australia by
    HarperCollins *Publishers*
First Intrigue Press edition, 2002

This book is a work of fiction. Names, characters,
places and incidents are either the product of the
author's imagination or are used fictitiously. Any resem-
blance to actual events or locales or persons, living or
dead, is entirely coincidental.

Library of Congress Cataloging-in-Publication Data

McLaren, Philip, 1943-
    Scream Black Murder: A WorldKrime mystery / by
        Philip McLaren.-- 1st Intrigue Press ed.
        p. cm.
    ISBN 1-890768-42-1
    1. Police--Australia--Sydney (N.S.W.)--Fiction.
    2. Australia aborigines--Fiction. 3. Sydney (N.S.W.)
    --Fiction. 4. Serial murders--Fiction. I. Title.

PR9619.3.M3266 S37 2002
823'.914--dc21

                                        2001052510

10 9 8 7 6 5 4 3 2 1

Acknowledgments

My sincere thanks to everyone who helped me develop this work: it is impossible to write a book of this nature without assistance.

First of all, I thank my wife, Roslyn, my first and last adviser—and my severest critic—without whom I would not be writing at all.

My thanks also to Colin Tracey of the Westmead Coroners Court, a friend from my distant past, Colin was diligent in detailing procedures followed by those in his office; and many thanks to various anonymous members of the Police Service for their candid advice on police procedures.

I thank the Aboriginal Literature Board of the Australia Council. The Australia Council, the Federal Government's arts funding and advisory body, financially assisted this author.

Finally, I must acknowledge Australia's Aboriginal people who are an everlasting source of inspiration for any writer.

Introduction

This is a novel in which all characters and incidents are taken from my imagination unless otherwise accounted for in my introduction.

Except for the killing of the Aboriginal man David Gundy, no deaths written about in this book actually happened.

The government practice of taking Aboriginal children away from their family and culture as written here is true. The Aboriginal Protection Act was passed by the New South Wales government in 1909 and its application only ceased in 1969. This Act was set in place to disenfranchise Aboriginal children permanently. The government hid children behind a screen of secrecy; they were taken to faraway places and made slaves, most working for no wages in white society. The children from the south were moved to the north while the children from the north were moved to the south. "Uncontrollable" Aboriginal children (those who reacted to being kidnapped) were kept in orphanage style homes until they were eighteen. They were then set free to fend for themselves with no knowledge of their families or their whereabouts and very little education.

Some who were educated were documented as illiterate to make servitude appear the best option for them. Although most children simply went "missing" there are some who were traced by family members and parents. Government documents verifying the action and indicating the offhanded manner employed in registering these children may be found at the State Archives of New South Wales in Globe Street, Sydney.

The ambivalent attitude of successive governments toward Aboriginal people is well documented: Indigenous Australians have the highest infant mortality rate, the lowest adult life expectancy, the highest incidence of blindness, the highest crime rate, the highest rate of incarceration, the lowest rate of literacy of any people in the developed world.

Redfern exists; it is an inner suburb of Sydney, which contains the densest Aboriginal population in Australia, one mile from the city center. I was born there in the front, upstairs bedroom of our two-story home on George Street.

Sydney

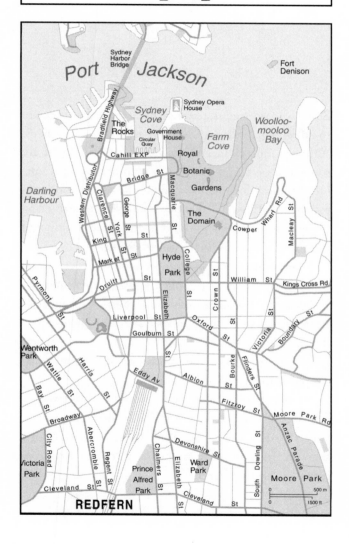

Port Jackson

Sydney Harbor Bridge

Fort Denison

Sydney Opera House

Sydney Cove

The Rocks

Government House

Circular Quay

Cahill EXP

Bradfield Highway

Woolloomooloo Bay

Farm Cove

Royal

Botanic

Gardens

Darling Harbour

Western Distributor

Clarence St

George St

York St

Bridge St

Macquarie St

St

Royal Botanic Gardens

The Domain

Cowper

Wharf Rd

Macleay St

King St

Market St

Drultt St

College St

Hyde Park

St

William St

Kings Cross Rd

Pyrmont St

Liverpool St

Goulburn St

Elizabeth St

Oxford St

Crown St

Victoria St

Boundary St

Wentworth Park

Harris St

Wattle St

Bay St

Broadway

Abercrombie St

Regent St

Eddy Av

Albion St

Bourke St

Flinders St

Fitzroy St

Moore Park Rd

Anzac Parade

City Road

Victoria Park

Chalmers St

Devonshire St

Prince Alfred Park

Elizabeth St

Ward Park

Dowling St

South

Moore Park

Cleveland St

Cleveland St

0   500 m
0   1500 ft

REDFERN

Redfern

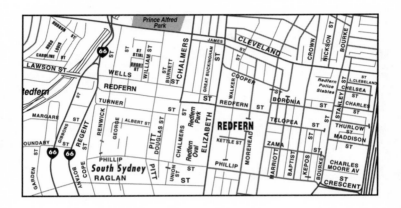

Greater Syndey

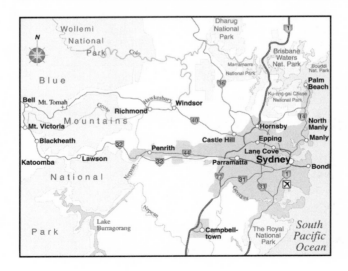

1

Human flesh decays five times more slowly when wet. The rain began at two in the morning; by three, the naked bodies, which lay in the shallow storm water drain beside the railway track, were half covered by a fast-running stream.

Long blue streaks flashed, leaving white comet trails as they crackled and peeled away from the overhead electric cables; the State Rail Authority's early morning passenger service was running on time despite the downpour. The train's headlights shone brilliantly white on the scene as it negotiated the gentle bend out of Redfern Station. The police flares attracted stares from passengers through the windows of the accelerating carriages.

The sweltering heat from the last day of the year had continued overnight and the rain fell, relentless.

The entire Aboriginal community from Eveleigh Street was assembled in the children's playground at the top of the steep rise near the railway tracks. They stood together, under umbrellas, in raincoats, or beneath large orange plastic sheeting. Two police-men prevented the crowd from moving nearer the scene while directing the curious in their slow moving vehicles to pass quickly.

A green unmarked police sedan with a flashing red beacon on its dash panel steered onto the foot-path, coming to a stop on a grassy patch beside four other police vehicles. Gary Leslie and Lisa Fuller, the full complement of the newly formed Aboriginal Homicide Unit of the New South Wales Police Department stepped gingerly out of the car into the heavy rain. They were met by an ashen-faced young constable with fast flowing rivulets running down his navy-colored cape.

"Are you Leslie?" he shouted to be heard above the noise of a passing train.

"Yeah." Gary nodded.

"Bloody gruesome sight. They're down beside the train line." He looked at the woman. "Are you with him?"

"I'm Detective Fuller—yes, we're together," she said, pursing her perfect orange painted lips in a crooked smile.

"Sorry, just go down by the fence at the end of the park. It's easier to climb down that way," he said. Then he moved away quickly to intercept curious newcomers to the crowd of morbid thrill-seekers who had now pushed forward, hoping to steal a glimpse of the bodies.

A rope had been erected as a makeshift balustrade to aid in climbing the grassy hill. Lisa held it firmly as she started scaling the steep slope to the wide concrete drain below. Partway down her fingers lost their grip on the wet hemp; grabbing the rope with both hands, she steadied herself and regained her footing on the slippery surface before moving on.

Gary followed, looking ahead at what lay at the center of the circle of police below. When he first saw the dead, dark-skinned bodies, his muscles cramped at the back of his neck. He winced and straightened his neck; his nerve ends had gone into spasm.

One of the detectives looked up to see Gary and Lisa approaching. He nudged another plain-clothes man who stood next to him. The two slowly waded through a deep puddle of water to meet them at the base of the slope.

"It's about time you got here," the taller one, Detective Captain Alan Jackson, said gruffly.

"Happy New Year to you too, Captain," Gary said.

"We came immediately," Lisa said.

"What happened?" Gary asked quickly.

"Two blacks, a man and woman . . . naked. He's

been shot twice in the head. There are no visible signs as to the cause of the woman's death. Not much more that I can tell you," Jackson said.

"Nothing's been found? No weapons?" Lisa asked.

"Nothing," Jackson replied.

There was a long pause as Gary and Lisa scanned the whole area. Jackson shuffled his feet impatiently then, finally, he said, "Well, we'll leave you with it. It's all yours, the two officers on crowd control can stay and we'll leave two more down here. How long will you be?"

"I'm not sure," Gary said, frowning.

"It should take you no longer than two hours . . . I mean, to clear it away," Jackson offered.

There was a pause. Lisa looked at Gary and raised her eyebrows.

"Okay, right . . . two hours." Jackson was uncomfortable but continued. "You've got radio and telephone haven't you?" he said as he prepared to leave.

"Yes, Captain," Gary retorted, his eyes drawn again to the bodies lying in the fast flowing water.

"Please remember, be thorough. It'll all go okay if you just take care . . . and be thorough," Jackson said. Then he waded through the water, past Lisa to Gary. He turned, looked directly into Gary's face and again said, "It's all yours."

Gary scanned the tall man's face as water dripped from the brim of Jackson's plastic-covered hat. The captain's gaunt face revealed lines deeply etched from too many years spent in a grossly understaffed department. He had seen a lot of death, a lot of misery; dead men and women, old and young, white and black; and children.

"Yes, Captain." Gary was serious.

A perceptible sign of relief swept across Jackson's face as he turned away; he had delegated the responsibility. He moved off then awkwardly pulled himself along the rope, up the slippery slope and over the knoll, out of sight.

"Two hours?" Lisa gasped.

"Take no notice of that," Gary said as he assumed control. "We'll establish our own pace." Now that Jackson, the executive officer, was gone, Gary became the senior officer at the scene: he was appointed two weeks ahead of Lisa.

He walked to the bodies, knelt down and touched the side of the young woman's head with the back of his fingers. The chill of death spread up his fingers along his arm and into his chest. Once beautiful and alive, she now lay on her stomach with her head to one side, her long hair flowed in the direction of the water, her lips dark blue. Her tongue had swollen, and now protruded grotesquely out of her mouth—it had turned a purple-crimson color. Her brown eyes were open; they had swollen also and bulged from their sockets. Her skin was incredibly wrinkled from the long immersion. The dead woman's head and right arm swayed rhythmically, gently moved by the water streaming by. It was an eerie sight.

From his quick scan of the woman's body Gary could see no visible sign of any cause of death. He watched as Lisa moved closer and used a pen to gently move the woman's hair from the back of her head. They both looked for a mark, a sign, anything.

The dead man lay three feet from the woman. He was on his back, naked, the left side of his head hit at least twice by bullets, which had entered near his ear. His legs were crossed in an ungainly pose. Definitely rolled into that position, thought Gary. He looked up the rise to the children's playground then walked nearer the two policemen. They watched him in silence as he surveyed the area, deep in thought. Lisa kneeled down for a closer look at the dead man.

"How long have you fellas been here?" Gary asked.

"A little over half an hour," said one of the constables.

"What's your name?"

"Ferguson and this is Humphreys," the constable

said, introducing his patrol mate.

"Right, okay, Ferguson, call the nearest station; ask them to send the coroner, his doctor and Forensic . . ." Gary looked up the steep rise again. ". . . and the Rescue Squad to get them up from here. Meanwhile see if you can build a dam that will run the water around the bodies, will you."

"Right sir," Ferguson replied.

"I'll call the station," Humphreys said.

Ferguson looked about for material to construct a weir, then meandered along the drain picking up odd stones and bricks.

"I know they won't like it but we need more men to search the whole area quickly, and we need to interview residents of the area to see if they heard or saw anything," Lisa said. "We can't do it fast enough by ourselves. We may lose vital evidence. This rain hasn't left us much as it is."

"I'll get the men," said Gary. He pulled a mobile phone out of the inside pocket of his overcoat.

Everyone at Headquarters had expected pressure from the media once the Aboriginal Homicide Unit took on its first assignment. The police service had reluctantly formed the new squad after considerable, consistent political pressure from the very vocal Aboriginal Legal Service. Too many black deaths went unsolved, they said. A lack of genuine concern by police and government amounting to blatant acts of racism, they said. Human rights groups and Amnesty International agreed. Momentum gathered further with the findings of the black deaths in custody inquest and had reached absolute fever pitch with the murder of David Gundy. The formation of the unit five months later was not well received by the established homicide squad or Alan Jackson.

Gary and Lisa had been asked to join an elite team of fifty carefully screened Aboriginal officers from all over Australia from which only two would emerge. They were given a ninety-day detective course at the police college. Lisa graduated a week before Christmas—Gary, three weeks prior to that. Now, on New Year's Day, they were assigned to their first homicide case. They knew they could not expect a lot of co-operation from the detectives in their section. The whole department felt threatened. They were already tarnished as racists by the media. Success by the Aboriginal unit at their expense wasn't something they wanted to assist.

The crowd in the children's playground above the railway line had grown considerably, forcing territory from the constables on point duty. They spilled along the rim of the slope where they could get a full view of the dead bodies.

Twenty minutes after Humphreys' call, a large, blue plastic canopy with State Police logotypes was finally erected over the bodies. Bright electric light was supplied, cabled in from an adjoining house and the swift running storm water was directed around the bodies. The coroner, his doctor, and a full scientific team of three worked hurriedly as fourteen uniformed police braved heavy rain, avoiding speeding trains to carefully scour the area in a hundred meter circle around the bodies; another six policemen were door-knocking. Two photographers—one from the police department, the other from the Coroner's Court—took pictures from every angle.

The coroner completed his work, stood and walked off towards the slope, conferring with his offsider. Two white-coated men approached Lisa as she stood beside the bodies, frowning, deep in thought.

"We'd like to remove them now, if that's okay?" one of the men said quietly.

"Oh, yes, wait. Just for a minute," she said.

She walked to Gary's side. He was busily trying to roll a cigarette. He looked up when she got near.

"Too wet. My papers are too wet."

"Have one of mine," she offered, pulling a packet from her purse.

"They want to take the bodies away. What do you think?" she asked him quietly.

Gary drew hard on the cigarette. "I suppose so. Christ, I hope we've thought of everything."

"We can ask them to wait for a while if you want."

"No, we should be okay. We've got videos and stills from every angle," he said.

"Plus we also have our collective memories," she added.

"Yeah, let's take them out of here," he said.

Gary drove slowly behind the unmarked coroner's van to the mortuary. It turned into a laneway, stopping at the rear entrance to the New South Wales Morgue. Someone opened the rolling metal door to the delivery bay; the van nosed inside.

Gary stepped out of his car. "Wait here. I'll check it out," he said to Lisa.

He hurried through the heavy rain into the delivery dock. Two men were lifting the blue plastic bags containing the dead bodies. Each bag had a zipper, which ran across the bottom, up one side and across the top. They look like my sleeping bag, Gary thought. He could see the heavy movement of an arm as a bag was lifted onto a stainless steel stretcher, which sat on top of a trolley. He walked beside the trolley as it was wheeled into a receiving area. Three bodies were being processed as they entered the room; the two new arrivals made five. Six policemen waited by the corpses as a large book containing information about the dead was hastily filled in.

"Where can I park?" Gary asked the short, moustachioed man who looked to be in charge.

"Around the front," he replied as he pointed out the route.

The smell wafting from the tiled rooms was something Gary would never forget. The back of his throat picked up the acrid odor; gagging he choked back the distinctive smell of decaying human flesh. It was like no other smell he could recall.

Lisa leaned forward to see Gary run out of the back entrance of the morgue as the old police car engine continued to idle irregularly and the windscreen wipers swished to and fro.

By the time they parked the car and found their way back along the wide corridors to the moustachioed man at the delivery bay, the two black corpses were all that remained to be processed.

The moustachioed man was quick and efficient. "Have you filled out your P79A yet?" he asked without looking up. He and a female assistant lifted the blue body bags from the trolley. They placed the lighter one on a large scale, then stepped back. "A hundred and thirty-five pounds," he called to the woman, who wrote it into the register.

"No, we haven't filled anything out yet," Lisa replied.

"Not to worry," he said cheerily. They placed the larger body on the scales and stepped back again. "A hundred and seventy-two," he called and again she wrote into the book.

"We'll send it to you as soon as it's completed," Lisa said.

"Today?" he asked.

"Yes, today." Lisa was firm, sure.

"Okay, I'll just get you to sign here and you can go," he said. "I'm Colin Richards and this is Pam Dundas." After Gary had introduced himself and Lisa, Richards continued. "We'll be doing your people this afternoon. Around two, I think. We've only had fourteen in this morning but it was a busy night last night, I believe, they took in thirty-two. Anyway, we'll be able to get to yours later today, okay?—after you get the forms to me." After a prolonged silence, he looked up. Recognizing he had rookies in his midst he asked. "Both new, eh?"

"Yeah," Gary replied. Lisa nodded.

"Don't worry, we're here to help and we're bloody well good at it too."

Lisa and Gary drove away from the morgue. Neither one said very much. Morbid details of the

day raced through their minds dimming out the
rest. Eventually, Lisa reached forward and switched
the babble of the police radio off and the regular
radio on. Country music filled the car; a cheery
female singer sang about how she had lost her man
then found him again, in full stereophonic sound.
Three traditional country guitars twanged and steel
brushes grated on a tight kettledrum. Vivid visuals
seen earlier in the morning flashed in and out of
their minds. Lisa switched the radio off; Gary
understood perfectly. He drove and they each dealt
with their thoughts in silence.

The rain had stopped, at last. The dark grey,
rolling clouds disappeared over the horizon. The
temperature rose five degrees in as many minutes as
the summer sun and a startling blue sky heralded in
the new year.

2

Lisa arrived home early. Alby, her husband, usually got in around seven from his city office. She sat nervously at the dining table. Alone she considered the pressure placed on her and Gary. They had agreed with the duty sergeant to split today's shift, enabling them to attend the post-mortem in the afternoon. She sat for several minutes, the sun streaming through the window, thinking what she would prepare for lunch. Nothing came to mind.

As an Aboriginal and a female raised in a strictly European, male-dominated society she recognized numerous obstacles placed in front of her from an early age but as she grew older she became more determined to overcome these obstacles and all prejudices against her. She clung dearly to her Aboriginality and, because she knew nothing of her family or clan, she felt robbed of the vital cultural connection to her language and land.

She wanted to help her people but she felt frustrated, powerless. In every area she thought she

might be able to help, the problems seemed insur-
mountable. For instance, she saw Aboriginal health
in urgent need of reform; reform in how it was
being delivered but even more importantly she saw
an urgent need to increase its minuscule budget.

She thought the gross imbalance of money spent
on health appalling. By using simple arithmetic she
uncovered an ambivalent government's attitude:
Australia's total annual health budget is $17,276
Million, the Aboriginal health budget is $99 Million;
from the Aboriginal figure $68 Million is set aside
for housing, sewerage, water supplies and power.
Other Australians have these paid for from other
portfolios other than health. So this left about $32
Million annually to spend on Aboriginal health.

Lisa deduced that if Aboriginal people repre-
sent 3% of the population it was fair they should
receive 3% of Australia's health budget, or $518
Million every year; and this figure should be spent
exclusively on delivering health services. But what
could she really do about it?

She learned that hands-on action could be found
in the police service and that appealed to her.

Lisa welcomed the heat from the sun through her
window. She remembered back to the warmth of the
winter's sun on her arms, when she was a child play-

ing with her old rag doll. Mostly she played in the backyard, on the front veranda or in her room but the day the big black car pulled up she was playing on the sidewalk in front of her house. She gave the car no thought at all, her old doll was more important. Brilliant sunlight gleamed from the car's abundant chrome work. It shone directly into her eyes, causing her to turn away.

Two men got out of the car and her mother met them at the gate. They handed her mother some papers, which she read. Lisa saw her mother become nervous. She began to raise her voice, she was angry. Lisa stood, scared.

Her mother turned toward her, her face distorted. "Run, Lisa, run! Out the back . . . go to Aunty Joyce," she screamed. Then she shielded the men from reaching her. But they easily pushed past.

Lisa realized they had come for her! She did as her mother said, with no clear idea as to what was happening, she ran. Her five-year-old body, fuelled by adrenaline, sprinted swiftly through the tall grass in her backyard. She squeezed through a small gap in the timber fence and continued running across a large cow paddock adjoining the house. She pounded her way up the side of Mrs. Watson's weatherboard house stretching her legs as she sprinted across the front lawn. As she reached the front gate, she panicked seeing the black car screech to a stop in front of her. She later learned the men were police officers dressed in plain clothes. One of them ran up behind her, threw both arms around her sweeping her off her feet. He forced her into the back of the car and slid in beside her. The car accelerated quickly down the dirt road.

Lisa began to sob. Huge tears rolled down her flushed cheeks. She had no idea why these men wanted to take her away her. What had she done wrong?

As they drove along the unsealed road, Lisa watched her mother run to the corner of her street; she was crying, shouting and waving her arms for the car to stop. It almost hit her as she stepped directly in its path. The shining vehicle weaved an "S" shape in the loose, red gravel before straightening again in the wide shallow drains at the side of the road.

"Jesus," the driver said. "That was close." He pulled at the steering wheel with both hands as he maneuvered the car back onto the road.

Lisa would never forget the haunting image of her mother's face, twisted with grief. The five-year-old could not possibly understand that she would never see her mother again.

Fried tomato sandwich with loads of butter and a glass of milk; she had finally decided on lunch. Why did she become a cop?—She is often asked. As well as it being a hands-on position, her enlistment in the police force was motivated by the large numbers of Aboriginal deaths that occurred while in police custody. Since she learned that Australian Aboriginals are the most incarcerated people in the world and the frequency of Aboriginal Australian deaths in custody to non-Aboriginals is documented at a ratio of eleven to one. Numbers don't matter to most people but they found their way into Lisa's mind and made loud noises. She imagined depressed black people, who rely on open space in order for their culture to survive, attempting to deal with shattered spirits and battered pride, forced to live in small claustrophobic cells for petty offenses for which few others are jailed.

Lisa's thoughts came back to the gruesome image of the dead bodies and the investigation. They had gleaned nothing from the door-knocking, and the garbage bag full of items removed from the area surrounding the crime scene was being closely scrutinized by Forensic but after a quick look it didn't appear they had turned up anything worthwhile.

3

Gary and Lisa's reasons for joining the police service were similar. He was furious that deaths of Aboriginal people were not investigated properly; also well-documented mistreatment and abuses by authorities were allowed to pass. The loss of black lives went largely unexplained. Gary told Lisa he could pinpoint the moment he decided to do something about it: 10.30 A.M. the day after he first heard the name, *David Gundy** and his death from a police shooting.

Gary used the time from the broken shift to pay some bills, writing checks. Sitting at his desk, pen in hand, rushing his arithmetic, reminded him of school. He even remembered the smells of school; the paint smells, musty books smells, rank toilet smells—he almost always waited until he got home.

Gary was nervous. He had a tenseness in his stomach and he needed to urinate. He held his mother's

*See Epilogue

hand firmly not wanting to let her go. She cheerfully chatted to him the entire 800 meters from their small terrace house to Cleveland Street School. He remembered that he feared growing up, growing apart from her, going to school. The closer they got to the old brick school the more children Gary saw. They were like flies around an open rubbish bin.

Inside, the hallways of the school were overlayed with glossy paint. On the walls hung large reproductions of Australian landscapes painted by Hans Heysen and Albert Namatjira, of gum trees dominating hazy, heat-filled fields. As he and his mother sat at the end of a row of wooden pews waiting for the headmistress, an older boy walked purposefully past, reached out of the second story window and pulled on a short, thick rope. Gary watched and listened as the heavy, old school bell mounted on the wall outside of the window tolled loudly, signalling an end to play and the beginning of lessons. The counter-weighted bell had an ornate trademark cast on its crown, testimony to its Scottish origins.

Gary stood and walked over to the nearest window. Children streamed into imaginary queues on the black asphalt. A teacher standing at the top of a long flight of stairs spoke to the children via a hastily positioned microphone. His amplified voice reverberated off old discolored bricks. "I honor my God

. . . I serve my Queen . . . I salute my flag." As he recited each short passage of the school pledge the children repeated it after him. Then they all snapped a crisp salute to the flag.

Gary's mother called to him along the hallway.

"Come on, love."

He turned to see her standing there with an older woman, the headmistress. Both women tilted their heads forcing over-friendly smiles.

This is it, Gary thought.

After further preliminaries in her office, the headmistress suggested that Gary's mother leave him with her. She could pick him up at three o'clock each day. As his mother bent to kiss him, Gary saw that her dark eyes were filled with tears. She almost ran out of the office. He felt a hollow feeling, grief, as his mother left him in the strange office.

Mrs. King was very friendly. Her large, yellow teeth pushed forward out of her mouth when she smiled. She gathered his papers and told Gary she would walk with him to his first classroom. She knocked softly on the heavy door, and then turning the brass knob, she pushed it open. A younger woman rose from the chair where she was reading a story to the class. Children were seated on colorful rugs scattered about the wooden floor. Everyone looked at Gary as he entered the room. The teacher lowered her head to Gary's face as he moved bravely ahead, gently guided by Mrs. King.

"This is Gary Leslie. He is joining your class today," Mrs. King told the children. "This is your teacher, Gary. Her name is Mrs. Graham." She stood behind him then gently pushed him forward with both hands.

"Hello Gary, come in. We were just reading a story about Jack and the Beanstalk. Have you heard it before?"

Gary shook his head from side to side while his right hand found its way to his face and pushed a shock of hair out of his eyes.

"Well, let's get you sat down and we'll continue. Then we can all find out what happened to Jack," she said as she looked about the room for sitting space. She took Gary by the arm and led him towards a group of boys seated on a large, Persian-style mat. The children shuffled as the teacher came near and made room for Gary to sit.

"Here we are, let's sit you next to John Wilson. John this is Gary, will you take care of him for me, please?"

Before Gary could sit, John cowered away and piped up loudly, "I don't want him next to me, Miss. He's a blackfella."

The whole classroom erupted with laughter. Gary

looked at the teacher, who didn't attempt to hide a wide smile, and then he looked at the headmistress who turned away to hide her mirth.

Realizing his remark had found an appreciative audience, John continued, "Blackfellas don't wash, Miss, their skin gets filled with dirt and it can't come out. That's why they're black."

Gary stood, his whole body swollen with anger. Tears came to his eyes as the laughter continued. He held up his arm for all to see and shouted, "I'm not black! I'm not dirty! You're dirty!" He ran to the loud, plump boy, John Wilson, and kicked him in the rib cage as hard as he could. The room erupted in squeals and yells. Gary dived at the boy, swinging wild punches in the general direction of his nose. Both teachers moved in and regained control but not before John's nose was well bloodied.

Gary put the checks into addressed envelopes and prepared to meet Lisa. He was frustrated that they had no insight into who would commit a murder of this sort, but he felt an urgency to catch the bastard.

4

---

*I watched the morning television news and listened
to the radio stations but they had nothing on. You
could usually get the first snippets of information
from them but the papers in the afternoon were the
best. They always had the best details and real good
photos that you could look at for hours, if you
liked.*

*The last one in the Blue Mountains was the best,
so far that is. Channel Eight's* Australia Today *show
gave it the most amount of time of any news item I
have ever seen. I taped it. It reminded me of the first
time. They all remind me of the first time. I suppose
it's like when you lose your virginity. You remember
it all the time, don't you? I do anyway.*

*I wasn't living in Sydney then. I was still going to
school up at Goulburn. God it gets cold in
Goulburn! Just because it doesn't snow there, people
think it's not cold. Having said that, I remember
seeing a photo taken in the thirties or forties with
snow on the main street, so it did snow, at least once.*

Well, I can tell you from personal experience, it gets very, very cold in the winter. That's how it was the first time; very cold, when I lost my virginity.

I'd watched her for days. She'd moved from Brewarrina, that's up in the north, somewhere way out at the back of woop woop. She wasn't what you would call black. She was brown—light brown, really. She had short, black, curly hair and small pointed breasts that were like cones. You could make a cone out of cardboard and stick them on her and you wouldn't notice any difference, with clothes on I mean. Without clothes on they still pointed straight up, even when she was on her back. She was my age, seventeen. We were doing our Higher School Certificate together. Well, she was in the same year as me but she was in with the real brainy kids. Not that I'm not brainy, I am, but she was a bit brainier. I wouldn't be able to do what I do and not get caught if I didn't have some brains, would I?

It was a cold day and sleet was falling, the day when I first talked to her. She was walking along the main highway, across the bridge near North Goulburn, to catch the bus to school. We caught it together after that. The wind was cold; it went right through my jacket, sweater, shirt and singlet. She said that she remembered me from school and that she saw me play football once. I was proud about that.

The next time I saw her was later in the day, at lunchtime. She smiled at me. I knew right then that I had to have her.

I followed her home from school. Of course I kept a long way behind her, so that she wouldn't see me. She lived in a nice old stone house near the railway line. Her father worked on the railways, I think. I'm not sure but I think he was a locomotive driver. I walked past a few times, and then I stopped in the park across the bridge and took out a book and pretended that I was reading. I watched her house until it got dark and the streetlights came on. She had lots of brothers and sisters—I couldn't count them all. They were coming and going all day. Must have been six or seven of them. So they wouldn't have missed Pauline hardly at all.

I watched her at school and at home for two weeks before I had the idea to take control of the situation. Masturbation was okay but I wanted some real sex, you know, with a girl. I thought that having it with a black girl would be much better than a white girl. They are closer to being animals than we are and it would be more intense. I wouldn't want to do it with a monkey or anything like that. I just thought a black girl would make it more intense, for my first time.

She sometimes did some shopping for her mother after school and that's when I met her, in the park. I was faking reading my book and she came by. I asked if I could go with her. She was a bit embarrassed but she said that if I wanted to, I could. We talked on the way there and I waited at the corner while she did her shopping then I walked back with her.

When we got to the other side of the bridge I pulled out my little .22 handgun and stuck it under her chin. Well I waved it at her first. She was really scared. Right away she did exactly what I wanted her to do. I was a bit surprised; I thought that if she screamed I would have to run off. I thought for sure I would get caught, but I haven't been.

I got her to make a turn one road before her place. We walked up along the road to the big war memorial on top of the steep hill, which overlooks the whole of Goulburn. It's lit up at night by big, yellow lights. We were both pretty puffed out when we got to the top. It was getting cold and dark. It was completely deserted. I made her climb the stairs to the lookout, balcony-thing at the top of the stone tower. It had turrets all around. I felt like I was in a castle in England or something and Pauline was my prized catch, my maiden, which she was.

I got her to pull the groceries from her shopping bag. There were a lot of things to eat, like bread, cheese and other stuff. So, I told her we would eat first. She was pretty scared and kept asking me not to *kill her, that she would do whatever I wanted. I wanted to eat first.*

It started to get cold so I thought that we had better have sex because I wanted us to take all of our clothes off and it was getting cold. I wanted her to take hers off first so I could have a good look. Her brown skin looked great. I got her to open her legs, roll over on her knees and push her arse in the air and everything. Her body felt beautiful and warm. Her pointed breasts stuck straight up in the air. I sucked on them for a short while. I asked her if it felt good. She said it did, but I didn't believe her. She was shaking and crying she was so scared. Then I got undressed quickly but I kept hold of my gun all the time. I was real hard. I got on top of her, between her legs and pushed myself inside her. It felt hot in there. I did it to her for a long time. When I came, I fell flat onto her and lay there for a while. She lay there quiet, still crying which was beginning to get on my nerves. Then it came to me that she was no virgin, she hadn't bled or anything. That put me right off. So I shot her, three times under her chin. It was more messy than I thought it would be; blood and stuff flew everywhere. She didn't know I was going to do it— I just did it quick.

It was poetic really. Pauline laying flat out dead at the top of the war memorial, which was a monu-

ment to the many hundreds of Goulburn men who were dead, and the big stone monument being their reward for killing hundreds of others. She was just one more dead. I didn't think it mattered. I still don't. She was black.

I took all of her clothes and all of the food and went home across the open fields. I burnt it all later.

It's true; you always remember the first time.

5

Evelyn Bates felt vulnerable walking to and from her work at the Black Dancers Studio. She lived in Redfern at the opposite end of Prince Alfred Park from the studio. During daylight hours she walked through the park along the old winding pathways, which weaved their way past the huge Moreton Bay figs. It saved her ten minutes. At night she hurried the long way around, along Chalmers Street.

The studio she danced at was situated on a corner near Central Railway Station across from a small green patch of parkland. The park was home to twenty pigeons and at least three derelict men. The hours she worked were irregular, ranging loosely from nine to five one week then twelve to eight the next. All the contract dancers were required to teach evening classes. Evelyn taught an adult class at night every second week.

She ran quickly between two cars as they moved in a slow line toward a red traffic light. One of the drivers yelled something to her, she didn't understand or care what. She guessed it was something obscene.

Once inside the coolness of the dance studio, a converted leatherware factory, she felt relaxed, at home. She put her head around the corner of the office door at the foot of the stairs. She had a compulsion to announce her arrival, reporting in was a discipline held over from her schooldays.

"Hello, I'm here," she called and waited for someone to acknowledge her. No one was in the office this particular day.

She walked into the lobby area, which connected three offices, dropped her kit bag and sank heavily into an old, leather chair. Posters of previous productions festooned the freshly painted walls alongside framed photo blow-ups of dancers in full flight. Evelyn was featured in two of the photographs. In one she was at the center of a group, topless, with her body painted in traditional style. The other was taken from a low angle beside the stage—it froze her at the apex of a mighty leap, her light silk costume streaming behind her as she flew, hair down her back, her chin upwards.

Muffled electronic music drifted along the corridor. Evelyn moved to the rhythm of the sounds. She was very black skinned, tall, thin, with long wavy hair that she usually tied back in one huge bunch. Originally from Yirrkala in Arnhem Land at the very top of Australia, she had been living in Sydney for years. From where she was seated she could see her own reflection in the glass panels of the double doors. She leaned forward, pursed and pouted her red painted lips and pushed at a frond-like strand of renegade hair, which had fallen free of her long scarf. Long earrings fashioned from wood framed the sides of her face. She wore a cotton Indian print, wrap-around skirt with an elasticised tube top, which pushed her breasts flat. Her dance gear, towel and toiletries were stowed in her Reebok carry bag.

The corridor music stopped. A door opened and several footsteps pounded on the bare wooden floor.

"If you work at more basic kinds of acoustic rhythms to assist the melody, it might suit a segment we are developing," Danny said. Danny Renaldo was the artistic director of the all-black company. His real name was Paul Ferguson. He was brown, stunningly good looking with a well-developed muscular body. He was gay. Classically trained in Melbourne in the Australian Ballet Company, he was *the* dynamic force behind contemporary Aboriginal dance.

Leading a small entourage he turned into the lobby. He spotted his head slightly, as all dancers do, as he changed direction. His face lit up when he saw Evelyn. "Hello darling," he said. Neglecting his four visitors, he reached out and gave her a long, full-body hug.

"Hello Danny," Evelyn said as she wrapped her arms around him tightly. "Mmmmmmmmm."

They had seen each other only yesterday.

"Please go ahead into my office, I'll be with you in a second," Danny said to his smiling companions.

When they were out of earshot he whispered to Evelyn, "Boring bands with their boring managers and boring agents." He squinted and wrinkled his nose. "But they do have one very smart piece that will go with our Black Space segment. So, darling, while I go and talk to them can you start our mob off with that new Unification music we worked through yesterday?"

"Of course," she replied. Then she bounced out of the comfortable chair while skillfully retrieving her kit bag.

"I'll be up soon," he said. "You're an angel."

Evelyn watched him walk to his office. Danny was always friendly but lately he had been too considerate, she thought. He was assisting her career enormously by allowing her more responsibility. And he didn't look well.

The large rehearsal room covered most of the top floor. It had a four-meter-high ceiling with full-length mirrors running the entire length of two walls; beneath the tall windows a long exercise bar occupied a third wall. The blond pinewood floor had been discovered under a layer of tired vinyl tiles; rejuvenated, it was perfect for dancing; with just the right amount of "give" under foot. On the far side of the large hall were change rooms, showers and toilets.

Evelyn undressed then pulled on a red lycra leotard over her black tights; afterwards she carefully laced on her small rubber-soled dancing shoes. She draped a towel around her neck and drank from a large bottle of Evian water. Then she stowed her bag in a locker next to her street clothes. Low angle morning light streamed through the wire-meshed windows. Evelyn could hear the voices of other dancers arriving as they climbed the stairs to the hall. Some of them shared houses or flats.

Evelyn preferred the privacy and flexibility of living alone, though she could barely afford it. She reached the exercise bar as they entered.

"Good morning all," she called to the group.

"Morning . . . morning . . . morning," they answered, as if musically orchestrated.

"Danny asked me to take the first session this morning. So, please join me here for stretching as soon as you can and we'll make a start." Evelyn was stimulated by the extra responsibility Danny had given her. She was now known as a beginning chore-ographer. Although still the principal female dancer with the company she knew it couldn't last forever, four, five, six years maximum, *if* she managed to overcome the inevitable injuries. Choreography offered longevity in her beloved business.

Two hours into the class, Evelyn called a break. The group had worked slowly at first, building in intensity as confidence with the structural flow of the new piece took hold. It was another hot day. Evelyn reached for her towel and her bottle of Evian. Danny had never left her with the company for so long before. She skipped her way gracefully across the wide floor and down the narrow stairwell to the office. Laughter echoed in the hall behind her.

Rosie, the Girl Friday, was busily taking a phone call while at the same time, she typed furiously. She looked up as Evelyn entered. Evelyn pointed to Danny's office. Rosie nodded and mouthed the words, "Yes, he's in there."

After gently knocking Evelyn let herself in. Danny sat with his high-backed chair facing away from the door and was looking blankly at the old wooden Venetian blinds, which blocked out the brilliant summer light. "Danny? Are you okay?" she asked quietly. He didn't answer. Evelyn moved beside him. Danny stared ahead, tears streaming down his cheeks. "Danny?" She fell to her knees and took him in her arms holding him tightly. He leaned his weight onto her and began sobbing. A letter lay open on Danny's desk from his doctor; Evelyn picked it up and read. Her worst suspicions were confirmed: Danny tested HIV positive three years ago, now he had full-blown AIDS.

Evelyn moved quietly from the room and scaled the stairs to the studio by twos. She explained Danny's bad news to the waiting students and asked if they wanted to leave early—they did. She went back to Danny in his office; they sat and talked about what he would do. At midnight they left together in a taxi bound for Danny's small harborside flat. Neither paid any attention to an additional resident of the small park opposite. He had joined the park residents the previous week and was very interested in Evelyn. He watched her closely as she entered and left the building. When she appeared briefly at the large windows he sat bolt upright. He had followed her and stood next to her when she bought lunch from the corner delicatessen two days earlier; he even learned her name.

6

By mid-afternoon people swarmed, insect-like, through the corridors of the State Coroner's complex. Eighteen people, including Gary and Lisa, crammed into a small autopsy lecture theater. Some were there in uniforms—police, ambulance—others were medical and nursing students. This wasn't something Gary or Lisa looked forward to. The dead young female Aborigine lay on the stainless steel bench. The bench wings were raised to prevent body fluids from splashing on the coroner's assistants as they systematically dissected the body. The first incision from ear to ear brought a loud groan from those watching, even the more hardened witnesses blanched; it was quickly followed by a long cut from the throat to the pelvic bone which allowed the whole upper body to be peeled open. The tongue, lungs, heart, intestines, stomach, kidneys, liver and bladder were removed and isolated. Then, separately, they were placed in jars filled with yellow fluid. Adhesive identification stickers were stuck to the glass containers, which were quickly wheeled away for analysis.

Colin Richards, the senior attendant, dictated into an overhanging microphone. After the dissection of the body was completed he concluded: ". . . there are no visible signs as to cause of death present at this time." He leaned away from the microphone and whispered to his female assistant, Pam, "Make arrangements for X-rays of the skull." He sought Gary out in the crowd, beckoning to meet him in an adjoining room. Gary tugged at Lisa's sleeve and took her in tow.

"I'm sorry; she hasn't given up her secret yet. But I have found something—one small lesion. Wait for the visitors to leave then come in. I want to show it to you."

The viewers chatted nervously as they were ushered from the autopsy theater. Gary and Lisa sat and waited for Richards. "She looks even younger than this morning," Lisa said.

"Yeah, just a kid," Gary replied. He looked once more at the body. The massive incisions made in the corpse were now being stitched closed. He was overwhelmed with feelings of reverence at the sight of the deceased female form in front of him as if he ought not be there at all. He allowed himself a few more seconds then diverted his eyes.

Colin Richards hurried into the room. "Right," he said. "Let's see. Come over here." Gary and Lisa were quickly at his side. He took the young woman's mouth, opened it widely and leaned her head way back. "Under here, on the roof of the mouth. Can you see it?" He took an instrument from a rack and pointed.

"Yes, it looks like a small cut," Lisa said. Gary agreed.

"I think it's a puncture mark from a dagger-like implement," Richards said. "I've called for X-rays of the head. I don't want to open the skull as yet because I might damage the evidence, if there is any."

They all stood back and Gary sighed. "When can we see the X-rays?"

"Oh, in just a few minutes," Richards replied. "We've got the male next door. You can appreciate he'll be simpler to do. You can come in the theater if you want but if you'd rather have a coffee . . . our canteen is just at the end of the corridor," he said, pointing along the hallway.

"Coffee?" Lisa raised her eyebrows at Gary.

"Yeah."

Once they were seated at a plastic table, complete with coffee and biscuits, Lisa asked, "Why would anyone ram a dagger in someone's upper mouth? It's a bit clumsy, wouldn't you think?"

"Bloody stupid, if you ask me," Gary replied. "But I suppose it doesn't matter how you do it, if you want to kill someone."

Lisa was curious. "People inject drugs in their mouths . . . so as to avoid syringe marks on their arms and legs, don't they?"

"I've heard of shooting heroin into the cheeks of the mouth but not into the palette. It would be too painful."

"But that might explain it? It might be drug related. She might be a prostitute on dope," said Lisa. "Her body fluids will soon show if she was on anything." She slid out of her cotton jacket, placing it on the back of her chair. "Let's look at what we've got?"

Gary shrugged. "Very little. . . ."

As they consulted their notes Pam Dundas hurriedly walked to their table. "Colin asked me to tell you the X-rays are ready. He has something interesting to show you," she said.

The X-ray room was in darkness as they entered. Richards had several light boxes switched on with X-ray films clipped to them. They clearly showed the Aboriginal girl's skull photographed from different points of view. He turned around as they entered; he had a smile of pride on his face. "She was shot," he said, positively, without reservation.

"How could that be?" Gary was quick to ask.

"Look, here," Richards said as he beckoned to them. "Can you see those white pieces? Here, here and here? While I can't be 100 percent certain at this stage, it is my best guess that they are fragments of a bullet. It entered her head at the roof of the mouth and hit the back of the skull, here, leaving a slight indentation. That is where the skull is thickest and at her age it is very strong. The bullet ricocheted off the bone leaving only a slight impression on the inside and nothing on the outside. Then, splintering into small pieces, the bullet bounced and flew around inside her head, each time passing quickly through her brain; she died swiftly. You can see, nothing has broken through." He looked up and moved his gaze from one to the other. "She had semen present in her vagina and anus. DNA testing will tell us if it is the semen from the male she was found with. She may have bruising to the arms and thighs but because of her very dark skin color we can't be sure. We can look under the skin if necessary but at this stage we feel certain there is bruising there."

"What about the male?" asked Lisa.

"As was clearly visible he was shot three times in the head at close range. A .22 caliber pistol was used. There was semen on his penis. His right leg was broken, which could have occurred when he was dumped and rolled down the slope beside the railway track. Now, let's see. All their vital items will go to various labs for testing. After we receive the results we'll prepare a summary and fax it directly to you. The coroner will need to meet with you some time after that, so, when we get it all together I'll phone you to arrange a time."

"There was no sign of a struggle? No scratches? No skin under fingernails?" Gary asked to be sure Richards had checked the obvious.

"I'm afraid not." He paused, thoughtfully. "Of course Forensic cannot confirm if the two bullets came from the same gun because one of the bullets disintegrated in the female's skull. My guess is they did, they were the same caliber."

Lisa and Gary were subdued. When the remaining formal exchange of documentation was over with, they slowly left by the rear exit. They drove back to the station, both silent, thinking.

Finally Lisa spoke. "Presuming the semen on our dead male and female don't match, we will have the killer's fingerprint, his DNA fingerprint."

"Yeah," said Gary glumly, "but what if they do match, and even if they don't, we've still got to find the bastard. Who's to say we'll have his DNA fingerprint on file."

He eased the car into the fast lane and sped towards headquarters.

Most detectives in the cramped office space at homicide headquarters stopped work to eye off the new recruits as they came through the swinging doors. One watched them conspicuously, a Greek-Australian called Mark.

Mark Poulos was born in Australia of Greek parents, neither of whom could speak English when they arrived. They stayed for seven months with his father's cousin after which time they bought their own home in Surry Hills.

Mark liked to wear gold. It contrasted nicely with his dark olive skin and black hair. He wore chains around his neck and wrists and several rings on his fingers. His watch was also gold. He was a tall man; his huge bulk suggested he spent time working out at the gym.

When Mark was seven and had started primary school, he was the brunt of every boy's joke and jest. He couldn't speak English very well; he wore strange clothing and brought unusual lunches to school.

His mettle was tested daily by school bullies and juvenile bigots emulating their parents. There was one, an Aboriginal boy, who came to his defense when the bashings started, Gary Leslie. Mark hadn't seen him since the fifth grade at Cleveland Street School but immediately recognized him as he walked the length of the room.

The much-publicized Aboriginal recruits, Gary and Lisa, had to run the gauntlet to reach their partitioned area, situated next to the toilets at the rear of the building. The sparsely furnished space had two phones, two desks, two chairs, two computer terminals, a filing cabinet and a wastepaper basket. A line of windows high overhead spilled sunlight into the large, musty-smelling room.

The previous day Gary had hung two large detailed maps of Sydney and New South Wales on the walls. He'd then placed bright orange fluorescent dots on them, marking unsolved Aboriginal homicide locations. The dots numbered 34. Today, they planned to access the police computer databanks on all 34 cases and transfer the information into a new cross-referencing program created to reveal minute correlations. They would look closely at sexually motivated murders of Aboriginal women, but more importantly whether any semen had been found and preserved. If so, they wanted it tested, DNA fingerprinted and compared.

The new recruits were unpopular with government bureaucrats because they were politically forced onto them. Their careers balanced precariously on a blade's edge, they needed to find the killer quickly.

7

I don't know why we have to copy American television shows in Australia but we do. This morning for instance, my favorite, the Australia Today show on Channel Eight, it's a rip off of a Yankee breakfast show. My stuff is becoming big news now so they sort of have to show it on all the channels but, like I said before, the Australia Today show gives the best and longest reports about my women.

This morning I was a bit hung over because I drank so much (heralding the start of the new year) but I dragged myself out of bed to watch Australia Today. The coverage was great, they sent a camera crew down beside the railway line and they even waited to interview the coroner after he checked the bodies out.

Gees, she was a terrific root, that black girl. Not at first though. But she kind of . . . got into it. I had to yell at her though. Let's face it, because, well, she didn't know me or anything. I wanted her when I first saw her working in that Aboriginal craft shop in Chippendale. She lived in Balmain and caught the bus to the shop every day. I really liked her craftwork as well. She did batik printing on soft silk fabric. I bought two pieces from her one day, a few weeks ago. I've still got them hanging on my wall.

She shared a house with two men and one other woman, all blacks. The other woman is not too bad either but Vera was a bit special. She had the character of a cat about her. She did her eyes as though she was a cat; she often wore leopard print clothing and her sexy lips she painted brown then rimmed them with a thin black line. She smiled at me twice on the bus. I began using disguises just before I started to follow her and the dancer. I got the disguise idea from the theater; they use all kinds of make-up and wardrobe to make the actors look different in the theater. In a way, I've become an actor too.

I never knew about theater gimmicks until I moved to Thirroul—I went to live there after I left Goulburn. I had to leave home; my mother and father were both on my back. Gees, I was a school kid and they kept nagging me about what I should do with my life. How did I know what I wanted to do? I still don't know and I've been working off and on for five years now. Anyway, I found out that people only look at what you wear . . . and that they never really look at you.

In Thirroul I joined an amateur theater group

that one of my mates from work was in. He said it was a good way to crack onto girls, so I went with him. It was good too, for girls I mean. But I didn't like many of them, except for Irene. Older women were okay but they wouldn't stay around long enough when we went for drinks after rehearsals. Some of them were married but that didn't stop them from grabbing a bloke if they wanted one. Irene kind of grabbed me.

Irene was married but liked us young fellas. I never saw her husband; if he let her stay out for all hours then he couldn't have been too interested in her, I reckon. Irene was only thirty-five, you'd think she was forty-five, her skin had toughened. She had deep squint lines in her face. Irene liked a bit of sex and made no secret of it.

I'm not sure that the cops ever found that black girl I shoved into the ocean at Bulli. That was one out of four of mine that didn't make it into the news. That Bulli girl had no idea I was watching her, for weeks I watched her before I grabbed her—it was my disguise. At the theater I played one of the kids from the musical Oliver; I used some of the make-up tricks to make me look like a tramp. I usually do it that way now. Women never look at drunken tramps; they just don't want to catch your eye. Now I'm on the dole I can play the tramp role with some convic-

tion—I haven't worked for nine months. Don't worry, I use different surnames as I move around, I'm not bloody mad. I use names of racetracks: Peter Warwick, Caulfield, Flemington, Wick, Farmer. I keep my first name though.

I know it's a bit conceited of me but I keep a scrapbook and a video library. I've collected clippings from the papers and I've taped all my Australia Today *reports. I like to read and watch the stories about my women. I have them in chronological order. There are four gaps in the full story though; I've been toying with the idea of reporting them one by one to the police. That's probably the only way I will get a full record. The police still don't know who the new ones at Redfern were. Too bad about her boyfriend, he chose to fuck her the same night as me. When I walked up to them they had just finished doing it on the grass. I shot him straight away. I burnt everything as usual.*

Soon after leaving Danny's flat at seven-thirty the next morning, Evelyn found herself standing in a bus crowded with peak-hour city commuters. She was still carrying her large kit bag, which created an obstacle for those leaving the bus. She was very tired. Danny had talked most of the night; she had been a good listener, his sounding board. He spoke to her of new plans. One of his ideas was to live in the country with his boyfriend. They might open a coffee shop or art gallery where he could wither and die out of sight. I'll leave them to remember me the way I was, he'd said. Or he might simply migrate to Northern Africa, never to return. She listened to him and cried with him. Now riding the stuffy bus she clearly recalled the despair in his voice; once more tears welled in her eyes.

"Are you all right dear?" a woman asked from the seat beside her.

"Yes . . . thank you," Evelyn said. She quickly turned away from the woman, dipping her head to peer forward at the road ahead. As her bus stop came into view, she depressed the red button on the upright chromium rail.

Evelyn skipped from the bus on her toes then scurried along the badly cracked footpath, settling into a brisk gait soon after. She was oblivious to the vagrant leaning from the recess of a nearby factory delivery dock. His body stiffened as he recognized her leaving the bus. He fell into step behind her at a careful distance. The blue and white bus disappeared amid a plume of burnt diesel oil.

"Tea or coffee?" asked Lisa. She stood and stretched, sighing as she felt instant relief from the pain across her back and shoulders.

"Coffee please," Gary replied without looking up from his PC monitor. They were both at their desks early every morning; feeling the full weight of their responsibilities, determined to live up to them. Already they had processed millions of pieces of information. Most of it appeared to be useless: seventeen women were brunettes, fifteen had regular boyfriends, three had cars, and ten worked in an office. They lived at varying addresses; there was no concentration of homes or crime scenes in one area. No patterns emerged. They must have lived somewhere with someone who knows them; surely they have friends and family, Lisa thought. But missing persons hadn't turned up any obvious correlations either.

"Sorry . . . I couldn't remember, tea wasn't it?" Lisa called across the large room as she walked back through the maze of desks. Her phone rang; she juggled the Styrofoam cups before picking it up. "Detective Fuller . . . Yes, that's right . . . How are you?" She pointed to her phone to alert Gary.

". . . It is as we thought," said Colin Richards from the Coroner's Office. "I've taken the fragments of the bullet from the girl's skull . . . we've completed our findings and you will receive a fax from us this morning with all of the information we have."

"Do you have a printout of the DNA results

from the semen?" Lisa asked.

"Yes we do. There were two specimens of semen found: one we have verified is from our male victim and the other is from an unknown male—it's detailed in our report. When you've read it please call me with any questions."

"Yes, I will, thank you Mr. Richards."

"Finally, there was some saliva and pubic hair present on the woman which matched the DNA semen. Our perpetrator's blood group is O-positive. Unfortunately that's not one of the rare groups but if our man has ever been to hospital he's almost certainly on our state-wide register."

"How many would be in that blood group . . . approximately?"

"Forty percent."

"Gee that narrows it down a lot." Lisa laughed.

"Well, you can halve that because half are female."

"This is true. Well thanks again Mr. Richards." Lisa heard his faint goodbye as she replaced the receiver.

Lisa scribbled some arithmetic on a notepad, sipped her sweet tea then jokingly made an announcement to Gary. "Well, we've reduced the number of suspects from four and a half million to nine hundred thousand."

8

Lisa was only five when she first saw "Bombala House" but she immediately sensed the terror it held for children. The verandas had military-style railings, which gave a feeling of being in barracks. The women who managed the hostel wore white dustcoats; looking back Lisa was abhorred that this automatically elevated them to medico status and that they reinforced this falsehood by insisting on being called "matron."

The girls ranged in ages from four to fourteen. All wore the same style dress: a white pinstriped cotton frock with short sleeves, a yoke of navy blue and a breast pocket on the left. The majority of the girls wore no shoes.

Barry Chapman was a red-haired schoolteacher who taught all thirty-eight girls in a classic one-room schoolhouse. With cane in hand, he was charged with making sure the children forgot their family, language and culture and instead learned the ways of the British. If they did, when they turned fifteen they would be sent away to jobs where they could earn good money. But mostly the girls learned how to scrub and clean.

When she turned eight Lisa's friends planned a surprise birthday party for her. It was to be held in nearby bushes where they had fashioned a playhouse. The girls built a yard around their cubby-house using a long line of rocks to mark the border. They swept the yard absolutely clean of any loose dirt, leaving a hard-packed clay surface. They confided in Mr. Chapman who agreed to detain Lisa while preparations were under way.

"Come to the front row please, Lisa," Mr. Chapman said. "I have some work I want you to help me with after school."

Lisa felt pleased to be chosen to assist the teacher and eagerly moved forward. Her friends giggled and left the room quickly as Mr. Chapman began to write on the blackboard.

"Could you please copy these titles on the front covers of that stack of books for me, Lisa?" he asked. "I need them for lessons first thing in the morning."

Lisa wrote, slowly at first, but becoming quicker as she familiarized herself with the task. She did not notice that Mr. Chapman had finished at the black-board and was standing beside her. His body swayed as he watched her work. The bulge in his pants brushed against her arm. She could feel the hardness of it as his sway developed a rhythm. He leaned over, breathing heavily as he put an arm around her shoulders, pulling her against him. She stopped writing and was frozen, scared. His other hand moved slowly under her dress, beneath her panties, between her legs. He moved more quickly now thrusting himself against her.

Lisa joined her friends at the bush cubby house a little later than expected. Her friends had gone to lots of trouble for her birthday. Crepe paper streamers and balloons hung from the bushes surrounding their cubby. They ate sweet biscuits, drank water and sang songs. All the children noticed how reserved Lisa was; it was her birthday, but she wasn't joining in. It was very unlike her. During the weeks that followed she became even more withdrawn, quiet and pensive; she feared being alone again with Mr. Chapman.

9

Gary looked away from the computer screen. "Let's get out of here," he said at last. "I'm going crazy, I'm hypnotized by this bloody monitor."

"Just let me enter this stuff . . . into this new program . . . and the machine can do some checking for me while we're gone," Lisa said. She rattled the keys of her terminal and pressed enter. It was done. She had accessed the new big daddy of all computers—the COPS—Computer Operated Police System. COPS was the latest computer program that highlighted minute pieces of information. As she leaped to her feet the computer murmured, executing her commands.

"Where to?" she asked, fumbling with the keys to open the door of the police car.

"Let's try Eveleigh Street." Gary's face was flat, unrevealing. "What did you ask from the computer?"

"You don't ask this computer anything. On the other hand, it tells you everything," Lisa said smugly.

Without speaking, Gary pulled the car out of the

police parking lot. He was deep in thought. As the car gathered speed he felt relief from the pressure of the office flow over him.

A row of twenty rundown tenement houses at the western end of Eveleigh Street had been purchased by an Aboriginal organization several years earlier and renovated for occupation by homeless Aborigines. They were all painted distinctive maroon and red colors.

Gary and Lisa knew the Redfern community had been thoroughly door-knocked, but now that they had pictures of the victims it might make some difference.

As the police car turned into Eveleigh Street, children scattered from their cricket game; the pitch was established in the middle of the road. An older boy picked up the rubbish bin, which was the wicket and took it over to the sidewalk. He then slinked into a house near the end of the street. Five men soon emerged from the house and walked to the middle of the street, blocking their way. Lisa stopped the car. The men moved forward, followed by all of the children.

"This is Aboriginal land. Piss off!" a tall overweight man called to them, waving his arms.

"And we're fucking Aboriginal!" Gary said as he opened the door of the car and leaped to his full height. Lisa quickly followed.

"We're investigating the murders of the Kooris found here last week," Lisa said.

The men ignored her and went directly to Gary. The tall one pushed his finger into Gary's chest. "We know what you are. Piss off!"

Gary grabbed the man's finger when it was pushed at him a second time and bent it back. In a reflex action the man threw a wild roundhouse punch. Gary easily slipped the blow aside, and still holding the finger, forced the man's arm behind his back. The other four men came quickly to his aid.

"Hold it!" Lisa screamed. The high pitch of her voice brought everybody to a halt. She held her handgun firmly; standing with her legs apart she looked down her extended right arm, and centered the gun sight on the tall man's chest. By this time people from all the surrounding houses had emptied into the street.

"Stop!" a thin white-haired woman called from her second story veranda. As if her words contained some magic, the group stepped back and quieted. "Harry, Joe come over here. You police, you come too."

Seated in the old woman's front room ten minutes later, Gary sipped tea from a small cup as he explained. "Look you've got to realize how damn lucky we are to finally get Koori detectives in this country. And in spite of what you've heard, we are *not* turning against our own kind. We are looking for murderers who kill Kooris. Whatever race the murderer happens to be makes no bloody difference to us."

"Yeah, but you think it's us who's done it. So you've come straight here, right?" the tall man said. He was Harry Williams, the manager of the Eveleigh Street Community Council. Harry had sung in a country and western band in Moree for many years before marrying Margaret Stewart and moving to Sydney with their three boys five years before.

"No, we don't. Let me tell you the truth," Lisa said. "We are at our wits end. We need your help. Some bastard is killing Aboriginal women. He rapes them and he kills them. This time the woman had a boyfriend with her." The room went still and quiet. Lisa lowered her voice. "Please, we're not getting anywhere, help us."

"Okay love," the old woman, Milsie Cain, said. "What can we do? . . . How can we help?"

Gary watched Lisa deal with the attentive group leaders. "We still haven't identified the bodies found beside the train line. I've brought some photographs of the victims to show you. But I must warn you, you may know these people, they may even be family. It won't be pleasant. Do you feel up to it?" They looked to each other then nodded and mumbled their agreement. Lisa pulled a thick packet from her coat and solemnly passed the pictures to the house-mother who distributed them. She and Gary searched their faces for any sign of recognition.

"I know this fella," Harry said suddenly. "He's from Taree. He's a R—"

"Robinson," Joe broke in. Joe Wilson had come from Taree two years ago. He knew the Robinson family very well. He pointed to the picture. "That's Lionel Robinson, Jesus!" He slid his bentwood chair back on the floral linoleum and went to the bath-room.

"What about the woman?" Gary asked. The room was quiet; the old lady shifted nervously on her chair. No one knew her. Gary thought it strange that she hadn't been reported missing yet; she must have workmates, friends, family. Maybe she was on a holiday and not expected home yet . . . it *was* the holiday season.

Outside a roar went up. The tin garbage can clanged loudly as the well-aimed, well-worn cricket ball struck its target—the children had resumed their game.

10

Gary was in his third week in sixth grade at
Parramatta North Primary School when he bowled
his first over in a serious cricket match. The sports
master had been so impressed when he'd seen him
playing in a friendly game in the school playground,
that he immediately recruited him into the side.

"Can you bowl?" asked one of the other boys.

"Yeah, not too bad, I suppose." Gary smiled
shyly.

"Give the new boy a bowl," said the boy. "Let's
see if he's any good."

Gary felt that all fifty pairs of eyes were on him as
the ball was thrown to him. He caught it very casually.

"Well, he can catch," said Mr. Alan, the sports
teacher.

Gary walked a short distance to allow for a
medium-length run-up. Then he came in, gaining
in speed when he gauged his run-up to be correct.
He tightened two fingers on top of the ball on
either side of the seam, placing his thumb under-

neath. His target was the left foot of the boy who was batting. When he reached the bowling crease he brought his arm over very quickly, delivering the ball with considerable skill. The batsman danced away as the ball came towards his toes, beaten by the sheer pace of the ball. It skidded under his bat and shattered the stumps amid delighted cheers from the boys. Gary had clean bowled the school's star batsman with his first ball. He soon became the senior team's new fast bowler.

But as the season developed, it was as a batsman that Gary really excelled. He enjoyed the challenge of batsman against bowler. And would pit his skill against anyone. He loved occupying the crease. Some days he would stay in all through his team's innings, scoring very few runs. On other occasions he would chase high targets. The brother of a former Australian Captain held the school record eighty-one not out. It was his record Gary decided he would own before he left the school at the end of the year.

Gary helped carry the cricket tackle kit the short journey to their match at Belmore Park in North Parramatta. Northmead, their opposition, had fielded a very good pace attack the previous year, Gary was told as they walked. He didn't mind facing fast bowling. He enjoyed nothing better than glancing the ball, using the bowler's own pace to score runs. It was a hot day, the new ball would move very fast through the air.

Gary asked the teacher if he could open the batting for this particular match; normally he batted one or two down the list. He explained how he liked facing fast bowling and he had just heard that two of the Northmead boys were very fast. Fifteen minutes later Gary found himself in the center of the ground facing the first ball of the innings.

Maxie Ellis's long straight black hair streamed back from his face as he ran in to bowl the opening over. His first ball was fast but wild, it went safely wide of the stumps. Gary watched it go by then lifted his bat feigning a late cut shot. He smiled back down the pitch at the bowler who was not amused. The second ball was even faster and swung in the air towards Gary's shins forcing him to bring his bat down to block it from hitting his legs. The ball rolled slowly back to the bowler from the dead bat. Now it was Maxie Ellis who smiled sarcastically as Gary struggled to regain his footing.

Gary watched two more balls go by; the next was short-pitched, not as fast as the others. He could see it as big as a football and he had plenty of time to pull his bat back, swing forward and follow through. The ball sounded sweet on the lower third of the bat then it raced past the bowler to the flags, which marked the boundary. His teacher, acting as umpire at the bowler's end, signalled four runs.

An hour and a half later Gary tilted his head back and let the iced Coca-Cola run down his throat. The drink break had been called early because of the heat. Gary had scored fifty-two runs, with the rest of his team adding only twelve for the loss of five wickets. The record was in sight so long as he didn't run out of partners. The five remaining players to bat were all bowlers. But he looked confident as friends encircled him, joking and smiling, giving their encouragement. Here was his chance to make it onto the pages of the school record book.

Maxie Ellis and Barry Douglas from Northmead were not in such a conciliatory mood.

The sounds of a hand clapping echoed across the field, signalling the restart of play. Gary walked slowly out to the center of the park. He felt a smile creep onto his face as he readied himself once again for the Northmead pace attack.

The first ball from Barry Douglas was predictable: fast and straight. It was aimed at his wicket but short-pitched. Gary cracked it to the boundary for four. The next came even quicker but it too was short pitched and he gave it the same treatment. The ball was thrown back to the wicket keeper via two boys as the bowler turned his back and walked to his run-up marker. Gary was now on sixty runs.

The well-gloved and padded Northmead wicket-keeper called encouragement to his bowler as he threw the ball back to him. "Come on Barry, this black boy has got to go . . . it's walkabout time." The whole team laughed.

"That's enough of that!" Mr. Alan looked furiously at the other umpire but the Northmead teacher shrugged in his direction. Gary's dark skin glowed, his eyes narrowed.

Inspired, the fast bowler came sprinting in. Gary was now even more determined than before. He danced down the pitch to meet the bounce of the ball. It came out of the bowler's hand much slower and totally deceived Gary. It went under the quickened stroke of the bat, narrowly missing the stumps. The whole Northmead team exclaimed at the nearness of the out. Gary shuffled nervously at his crease. The wicketkeeper retrieved the ball and threw it back to the bowler.

"This nigger's going," said the wicketkeeper. His teammates laughed loudly, impressed by the defiance of their school friend. The teachers looked to each other.

"There will be no more of that Ronnie," the Northmead teacher said finally.

Gary watched the next ball carefully as it went by, and the next and the next. He had lost his momentum.

"Over!" Mr. Alan called the end of the bowling spell and the team changed ends.

Gary remained at his batting crease and the Northmead teacher came next to him to officiate at the stumps for the next over. "He's got you worried now, hasn't he?" he said to Gary through his teeth without moving his lips. Gary stepped away from him as Maxie Ellis came in to bowl.

Michael Jones was batting at the far end. He flayed his bat awkwardly at the speeding ball, which brought a few giggles plus the usual "ooos" and "aahs" from the boys as it narrowly missed the stumps. The next ball shattered the stumps. He was clean bowled! Gary's hopes of a record were fading. Five balls later Ray Carlisle was out; Gary hadn't been able to get to the batting end at all.

"Over!" shouted the Northmead teacher. "You're next to go, you little black bastard," he whispered to Gary as he turned away. Gary was stunned. The field settled down as Barry Douglas careered forward to bowl.

"Come on Barry, this dirty Abo's no good . . . Take him out," the wicketkeeper called across the field. Gary threw his bat down and turned on the boy whose face drained. His mouth fell open as Gary grabbed him by the shirtfront. He positioned him carefully and let a tightly closed fist fly into the side of his nose. The crack could be heard across the field. Blood streamed down the front of the boy's white shirt.

"I don't have to put up with idiots like you . . . you pig-faced racist!" Gary yelled as he hit him hard on the jaw. The teachers pulled Gary away and after a heated conversation agreed to the match being drawn. On the way back to school Mr. Alan kept patting Gary on the back, telling him over and over that it was not his fault. Gary never played cricket again.

11

Evelyn slowly sank into her hot bath. The water stung the skin at the back of her thighs and buttocks but it felt good. She gave out a loud gasp then inhaled the steam and smelled the scented soap bubbles. She slid along the bottom, lying on her back, pushing her shoulders against the gentle sloping end of the tub. Exhausted, she closed her eyes. The water lapped against her chin in the deep, old-style bathtub. The pipes in the walls clanged and shuddered.

After a while Evelyn heard a soft knocking. She wasn't sure if it was at her door or not. She didn't care, she wasn't moving from this position. There it was again, more knocking. It sounded like an animal, a dog, or something, curling up on her doorstep.

Evelyn allowed the water to run into her ears as she lowered herself below the surface. Still with her eyes closed, she could hear music in the distance. Her thoughts drifted to the dancing and Danny.

She was in awe of Danny when she first came to

work under him. She was from a small community, part of a clan who still had their language and land. Danny not only hired her into the dance company but also took a personal interest in her while she coped with big-city living, until she felt comfortable and confident. Her people still hunted and gathered as they had done for centuries, as she had done before she came to Sydney. The lifestyle change was very dramatic indeed. But that was years ago. And now, Danny had become a close friend to her, one who she cared for deeply. She was very worried about him.

The knock at the door was louder now. It was no animal. But Evelyn was expecting no one and would not admit anyone to her sanctuary this morning.

The vagrant knew she was there. Why wouldn't she open the door? He had carefully calculated the kind of knock he would use. He didn't want to bang too loudly. He wanted to show her his gentle side. He had so looked forward to meeting her today.

12

Gary's electronic alarm clock bleeped the beginning of his day. He woke wide-eyed and quickly sat upright. Helen, his wife, crooked her neck and spoke softly. "Okay love?" she asked.

"Yeah," he said.

"Did you get enough sleep?"

"Yeah. I'm okay. I slept well."

"It's a long drive." She knew he hadn't got to bed until midnight.

"I'll be fine."

Helen got out of bed anyway. She couldn't let Gary go to Taree without helping him on his way, no matter if it was four in the morning.

Gary and Helen were a good match. They had met three years before at a dinner party which both had attended with other partners. They had gotten along well and laughed a lot; she actively pursued Gary for weeks afterwards. He was flattered, of course, but was enjoying his relationship with Patricia, an arts student at Sydney University whom he'd been seeing for the past six months. Helen's dinner-date had been a friend's brother who was a mate but not a potential lover.

Gary held his face up to the shower allowing the warm water to run down his body then he turned the hot tap off. The cold water chilled his body. He remembered how his swimming coach had told him to always use cold water at the end of a shower. It closed the pores of your skin, preventing infections and disease. The smell of freshly brewed coffee wafted throughout the house from the kitchen.

Gary had had mixed feelings when Patricia's research grant—requiring a seven week stay in Paris—finally came through. But it cleared the way for Helen who had schemed, patient and attentive as a girl can be at telephone length. They married a year later. Helen's third generation Irish-Australian father and second generation English-Australian mother were not certain at first about their daughter and her Aboriginal husband. But three years later they had witnessed how their love had blossomed and with the birth of their wonderful grandson, David, all the barriers were down.

Alby, Lisa's black husband, sat in bed and watched Lisa dress. He didn't like the idea of his wife going away for seven days with a man. He had met Gary briefly and liked him well enough, but if he had chosen someone for his wife to spend a week with it certainly would not be him. Gary was all of the things he wasn't—a sportsman, a successful career man, well spoken, confident, tall and handsome with the whitest, most perfect teeth in Australia.

"You're beautiful," he said, as she stood almost naked. "Will you call me . . . or do you want me to call you?" he asked.

"I'll call. You may not catch me in my room," said Lisa, smiling despite her tiredness.

"Is there any chance you will be gone for longer than a week?"

"I don't think so. There is an even chance it will be less than a week." She turned and smiled again. "Don't worry . . . it'll go quickly. I'm not going on a holiday you know."

"I know. I just wish I was going with you."

She had already packed her suitcase. Adding a few pieces from the bathroom she zipped it closed, carried it to the front door of the one-bedroom, high-rise apartment then stood, thinking. "What have I forgotten?"

The intercom's loud buzzing broke through the still, early-morning quiet. Alby came from the bedroom and swept Lisa into his arms then they kissed and hugged tightly. The intercom buzzed again. Lisa broke free and grabbed the receiver. "Hello Gary . . . I'll be right down," she said.

"No hurry," he replied.

As she replaced the phone piece, Alby came up from behind and wrapped his arms around her. His hands ran over her hips and under her short dress. She turned and they kissed again.

Gary lifted Lisa's sole suitcase into the boot of the car, next to his. They were both cheery, despite their tiredness and the stress and worry of the case. A holiday atmosphere prevailed today. Suddenly they were on the Sydney Harbor Bridge heading north. With very little traffic on the road their estimated travelling time to Taree was about three and a half hours. Lisa clicked the radio on; music filled the car. She slid down into her seat and relaxed into the long trip ahead. Gary picked up on her mood and relaxed his body for the long drive to Taree. The green Ford Falcon crossed the normally busy, five-way intersection at Crows Nest and sped north against the larger flow of incoming city traffic. The eastern sky had taken on a lighter blue, glowing orange at the horizon; stars were still sparkling across the clear western heavens.

13

I only wanted to talk to her. I didn't want anything else. Evelyn should have opened that door. She's really starting to make me fucking angry.

I've worked out another disguise to use. I was just playing around the other day with my theater make-up when I sort of found how to make a false nose. So I bought a wig and used my new nose and, geez, it made me look really different, really ugly. Women don't look at ugly men—I certainly didn't want them looking at me. At least not until I really want them to look. I tried it out yesterday. I went to the supermarket in Redfern. There were lots of blacks there, crawling with them. It is an excellent place to find women. My idea worked real good. No one looked at me—I was too ugly.

I went to the football last weekend, to watch the Redfern All Blacks. The Abo women go crazy at these games. They get a little loaded and they go crazy. They throw things, shout abuse at the poor bugger who is refereeing the stupid game and wait for him when he comes out of the dressing room to go home. It was fucking hilarious. I saw some good-looking women there too. But it all just shows how good Evelyn is. She has real class, for a black that is. When she walks it's like a ballet. I want her real bad. I haven't been this horny for ages. I'm going to pick up someone at the pub tonight just for a root in the meantime.

I mailed a package containing information about one of my girls to the cops. You know, to kind of help them along. I want to bring my media collection up to date, after they find her, like.

14

Ten-year-old Lisa felt a great weight had been taken from her—Mr. Chapman had been transferred from Bombala House to an ordinary state school in Sydney. He had not bothered with Lisa after that one time, he now favored older girls.

Although her schoolwork had slipped she still maintained high marks in all subjects. Last term the Bombala children had sat the same exam the local State school children and she had shone brilliantly as Bombala House's most outstanding student. She had beaten most of the town children her own age.

Lisa mixed with three older girls, Brenda and Lizzy, both twelve, and Beverly, who was fifteen. Brenda had grown boobs over the past year and already had her period but Lizzy had not yet experienced either. Lisa felt she was a teenager. Her older friends steered her reading towards more interesting books. They enjoyed reading the *Woman's Weekly* magazine together. They took great pleasure reading about city people—the way they lived, the products

that were advertised to them, the stories, the scandals
. . . It was a dream book for these young Aboriginal
children just as it was for most of its white, adult
readership. Their impressionable minds were
already thoroughly manipulated; they were now
ignorant of their own culture. The government's
behavioral control program for assimilating
Aboriginal children appeared to be successful.

Despite her relief at Mr. Chapman's departure,
Lisa was feeling sad. It was rumored that Beverly, who
was the oldest girl at Bombala, was to leave the following week. The staff had found her a live-in position with a family. A grazier, his wife and five children wanted someone to work on their property near
Nyngan. It was said the property was very isolated.

When the time came for Beverly to leave, tears
flowed freely. The girls were tightly bonded at
Bombala. They had fashioned their own all-female
family; for most it was all they had. Outside the gate,
standing next to the taxi that would take her to the
railway station Lisa closed Beverly's hand on a note
she had written to her.

As Beverly was driving away, amid dust and tears
and cheers, she read it.

Dear Bevvy,
Lucky you to be out at last. Free to explore

life. I am so excited for you. Good luck! Please
write to me. I love you. You are my best big
sister and I will miss you terribly.
Love always,
Lisa.

Gary grabbed Lisa by the wrist and gently woke her;
she had been asleep for ages. Almost exactly three
and a half hours after leaving Sydney they were
crossing the steel bridge which spanned the
Manning River. They turned into the main street of
Taree. The town looked green, clean, very busy and
prosperous.

"Sorry," she said. "I was exhausted."

"That's okay, we're here," Gary was pleased to say.

"That didn't take long, did it?" Lisa said as she
stretched her limbs.

"Well no . . . not if you slept all the way."

"I didn't sleep all the way."

"No, just the last hundred and fifty kilometers,"
he joked. "What do you say we go to our motel
first?"

Gary drove the car under an archway with a sign
on it that read RIVER VIEW MOTEL. They checked in
and walked off to find their adjoining rooms. Each
suite overlooked the river—the brown water carried
silt from upstream where it had been raining for the

past two days. The motel color scheme looked like something from *Miami Vice*: everything was painted pastel pink, blue and green. Agreeing to meet in the coffee shop in fifteen minutes, both disappeared behind matching pastel blue doors with a large seven and eight on them; the numerals in a typeface popular in the fifties.

The Taree police station was the local government architect's idea of modern. Lots of glass, local river boulders, cement, local timber with an environmentally friendly corrugated steel roof featuring a solar hot water heating panel. Gary and Lisa found the all-white police force friendly enough. They were accustomed to Aborigines here; with a local black population of fifteen hundred it was not surprising. They gave Gary directions to the Robinson family home.

Gary and Lisa drove slowly along a narrow residential street at the northern end of the Taree township. Most of the houses were clad with fibro—asbestos sheeting—and had red galvanized tin roofing. All were in need of repair.

The Robinson family had already been notified by the local police of Lionel's death. As Gary pulled the car to a halt in front of the Robinson house he pulled in a big breath. "I hate this," he said.

Lisa agreed. "Me too. Let's get it over with."

The door was opened by a dark teenage girl carrying a baby on her hip. "Yes, what do you want?" she asked.

"We're detectives from Sydney, we're here investigating the death of Lionel Robinson," Gary said.

"Yes, okay, come in," the girl said. "Mum, police!"

She directed them to sit on a small divan. The Robinsons were poor but house-proud. The floor was covered with colored vinyl; the walls were painted light blue. Lionel's mother was obviously suffering her loss badly.

"Mrs. Robinson?" Gary asked.

"Yes, that right," the old lady said.

"I am Detective Leslie, this is Detective Fuller, we're here to ask a few questions to do with your son's death. Are you up to it? We can come another time."

"No, I'm okay," she said. "What do you want to know? What can I tell you? I wasn't even in Sydney at the time. I haven't been down there for ten years."

Gary and Lisa began their questioning slowly; they found out that Lionel had not been living at home for a year. They gathered as much background information as they could about him but it was very superficial: jobs he held, schools he went to, places he liked go to, things he liked to do. They said they might be able to find someone from these places that would link him to the killer.

Gary continued to question the shaky woman. "When the local police informed you of your son's death, did they also tell you that a young woman was found dead beside him?"

"No, I didn't know that."

Lisa was quick to ask. "Can you recall him speaking of a girlfriend? A name, any name?"

Mrs. Robinson said, "Oh yes, he had a girlfriend, Vera, Vera Turner."

Lisa pulled a photograph of the dead woman from her case and showed it to the woman. All those in the room came for a closer look.

"Is this Vera Turner, Mrs. Robinson?" Lisa asked.

"Oh dear!" she said. "Yes, that's her."

15

All the River View Motel rooms smelled of chemically manufactured lemon. Lisa fell face forward onto her bed after a long, arduous day visiting four Aboriginal communities. They were all government housing development projects; small, hastily built, fibro and brick veneer homes. Each site was deliberately located well out of town, where the "problems" were manageable, containable and more importantly, segregated and out of sight. Most of the roads they travelled were sealed except for one stretch, which had a very loose dusty surface.

Lisa ached for a long hot shower, but she needed to summon her energy first.

Gary pulled off his shirt, picked up the telephone, dialled Helen at home then reclined on the bed. The air conditioner hummed and shuddered.

"Hello baby, how are you both?" he said.

"I'm fine, David's fine. How are you?"

"I'm good."

"How's the trip? Is it going okay?" Helen sounded chipper.

"We had a long day on the road. We found out who the girl was early this morning. She was from this area, too. So, we spent the rest of the day talking to people who knew them both. You know, getting background details. Where they went, what they did, what kind of people they were. They hadn't been living in Sydney all that long. Redfern is full of Kooris who are just passing through. That's why we are up here. This is where they lived most of their lives. Anyway, it's going okay." Through the thin motel wall he could hear Lisa taking a shower. He imagined her naked and wet. "We still have a lot of things to do up here."

"How long will it take? Can you gauge it yet, or is it too early?"

"Too early."

Lisa let the water flow over her from the top of her head. Her hair clung to her neck and shoulders. She turned up the hot water.

"Mum called this morning. She wants us to go over for a barbecue on Sunday, if you get back. Everyone will be there—Anne and Peter, June and the girls, Michael, everyone."

"Well, it's too early to know for sure."

"But it is the weekend."

"I know that but we can't come all the way home

Friday then back here for Monday. We have to finish our business here first."

"How is Lisa taking all this?" Helen asked.

"Lisa. What do you mean? She's okay. I suppose."

Lisa stepped from her shower and took a towel from the wall rack. As she dried herself, she could hear Gary's muffled voice. Must be on the phone, she thought.

Later that evening Gary knocked at her door. "It's only me," he called. They had already agreed to eat at the brightly lit Thai restaurant across from their motel. As they approached the blazoned red and green building Lisa looked at Gary. It was the first time she had ever seen him as a man. He was usually someone she worked with. Tonight she saw him differently.

They related to each other very well. Gary could talk to Lisa and she could confide in him.

"I suppose Helen keeps a fairly tight rein on me but I don't mind. We go everywhere together," he said.

Both detectives became more aware of each other as they sat face to face. Eye contact was comfortable for them both; they enjoyed the closeness across the small table.

"You've not been married for very long have you?" she asked. She knew the answer.

"Five years. What about you?"

"Alby and I lived together for a while before we got married. So, we've been together for about four years." she swayed her head sideways while she calculated. "Yes, four and a half years next month. But married for only two."

A slender Thai waitress appeared at the table. "Would you like some wine with your meal this evening?" she asked serenely as she presented menus with slow, well-rehearsed, balletic movements.

"Yes we would," Gary was quick to respond. In the dim light he saw a warm smile widen on Lisa's face, which, coquettishly, she partially hid behind the large red menu.

Strange sounds startled Lisa from a deep sleep early next morning. Unable to continue her sleep, she reached for the television remote control unit, which lay next to her on the bedside table and pressed the on button. She flicked through the channels: cartoons, kids' shows...then the *Australia Today* program flashed on. She yawned as she watched a boring interview about women not being accepted for more jobs at the steel plant in Wollongong. Several minutes went by then came the news. The newsreader wore a serious face as he read from the auto-cue machine: "Detectives this morning found the body of a partially clothed woman in

bushland at Lake Parramatta. Reports indicate
police were tipped off by an anonymous package
containing details of the site. They uncovered the
body near the water just meters from a popular summer bathing spot. We take you live to Channel
Eight's Maureen Moore who is at the scene.
Maureen. . . ."

The telecast switched to the camera crew on location. Plastic-faced Maureen Moore was profession-
ally perfect. She smoothly assumed a pose, missed a
beat then went into her rehearsed spiel. "Good
morning, Ross. It's a somber mood here at Lake
Parramatta with the discovery of the body of a young
woman. At around eleven last night police took
delivery of a package containing information alert-
ing them to search this particular area of the lake
resort. As you can see police have cordoned the area
off and are still looking for any evidence that might
assist them in their investigation."

Noisy activity behind the journalist caused her to
stop and look around. "Wait, something is happening behind me. Yes, Ross it appears they are now
removing the body."

The scene looked all too familiar to Lisa: the
police, the blue checkered plastic cordon, coroner's
officers, photographers, body bag. As they clam-
bered up a small rise, one of the stretcher bearers

lost his footing. The body fell heavily, dislodging the zip on the body bag; although shocked, the female reporter excitedly continued:

"Oh my God. An arm has fallen out from the body bag. That's awful. No! They're spilling her out. Oh my God! Oh my God!"

Lisa could clearly see the body of a young Aboriginal woman.

It was on TV this morning, I taped it . . . it was brilliant, bloody brilliant. They found her. I had to help them though— I sent them some stuff. But, Christ it was brilliant! She fell right out of the fucking bag!

Lisa and Gary's Taree tour of duty was abruptly cut short. They'd only had one full day, but it'd been productive.

The northern part of New South Wales was covered by cloud and it rained for most of the return journey. Lisa drove directly to Parramatta. It had stopped raining when they pulled to a stop on the lake's foreshore. A small forensic crew still occupied the site. They told them they had found a badly decomposed body, which they took to the morgue. Gary pulled back on his cigarette, deeply inhaled then let the smoke slowly escape as he walked behind Lisa along the embankment of the deep lake.

There could not be anything of any consequence left here, Gary thought. They would examine the area anyway. A strong smell of eucalyptus emanated from the trees surrounding them. The ground was soft underfoot. Gary walked further along the lake's edge. He had swum in this lake many times; as a twelve-year-old he lived a short walk from here. He looked back at Lisa bending over the grassy area where the outline shape of a body was painted. She was closely examining the ground. He walked further still, he felt pulled, attracted by a magnetic force. An eerie chill washed over him. An uncomfortable, indeterminable difference of mind made him turn and look across the lake. There, a hundred meters away, stood a man in an upright, defiant pose, his legs were wide apart; both hands on his hips. He was smiling. Gary looked to Lisa then back but he was gone. "You bastard. It's you!" Gary said out loud to no one. The man disappeared into the bushes.

Later that day, Colin Richards hurried into the large autopsy operating theater and stood beside his assistant. The stainless steel flaps on the sides of the table were up; from where Gary stood at the door, he could not see all of the female corpse. First the T-shirt was removed and placed in a plastic bag. A sharp, acrid odor emanated from the lady. There was some discussion between the two workers as they proceeded. Sounds of liquid and organs escaping from the corpse made Gary turn and walk back to the receiving area where he had left Lisa.

"Two shots to the head," Richards said as he came from completing his examination on the young Aboriginal woman. He walked quickly and beckoned for the concerned detectives to join him. "We know who she is. We've had a positive I.D. from a relative," he read from a sheet. "Yes, her brother it was. It was a wonder he could tell. She was badly decomposed, but her face did hold up well. She's been on our Missing Person list for quite some time. Her name was Maggie Crawford. I've got her details in my office." The three shuffled along the wide, white-tiled corridor.

Sitting in his office, Richards elaborated. "She was raped and shot before she was taken to the lake. We can't be sure about the date or time of death because she was so badly decomposed, but we estimate it was between two and three weeks ago. Her arms, legs and neck had been bound. The gunshot wounds created a wide opening at the side of her head. There were no bullets in the body or at the scene. You could expect a lot of bleeding from such wounds, but there was very little blood at the site. Let's see. We found some fibers on the back of her T-shirt. She was probably dragged over some carpet.

This type of carpet could found in a car or van or in a house. We will determine the type, color and manufacturer later today. There was an abundance of semen present, indicating several ejaculations."

"Have you checked the DNA print-out to see if it matches our other sample?" Lisa asked.

"Yes, I've already made that request. You'll have my faxed report as soon as it hits my desk."

"Do you have the brother's address, please?" Gary asked.

"It's right here." Richards reached into the manila file folder and pulled out a four-page form and read from it. "Colin Crawford, 51 Hassall Street, Parramatta. No telephone."

Later, as they drove down from the elevated end of Hassall Street, Gary finally told Lisa. "Look, I think I may have seen him today."

"What! When?"

"I'm not positive about it, but when we were at the lake. I was drawn a long way from the site."

"I noticed."

"Yes, well . . . a force, a magnetic force tugged at me, pulling me along the shore. My head turned involuntarily and suddenly there he was, smiling at me from the other side of the lake. He had a . . . psychotic smile. Disturbing, you know, legs apart, hands on hips."

"Jesus!"

"Exactly. The classic return-to-the-scene syndrome. It felt a bit bloody spooky, I tell you."

"No kidding?"

"I think we should keep a few men there to whet his appetite. We'll stake it out."

"You should get an Identikit done right away."

"It *is* only a hunch."

"I don't care. It's a scientific hunch."

Gary hesitated for a moment, and then said, "What do you think about us doubling our efforts by splitting up? Work separately on the stakeout, you know. We'd be able to cover more territory?"

Lisa felt abandoned. "If you want to. Sure. Okay. But you don't want us to work alone all the time?"

"No, just while we're on the stakeout. Then we can see how we go.''

"Good idea," Lisa said, understanding now and feeling more comfortable with the idea. "Jesus, you saw him."

They got out of the car at a house with 51 painted crudely on the letterbox and walked to the front gate. Gary reached out and took Lisa by the forearm to help her up a high step. She turned her head and looked at him. "Sorry," he said, quickly withdrawing his arm.

No useful information was gleaned from a lengthy interview with the Crawford family. They were asked about Maggie's habits, jobs, friends, boyfriends, places she frequented, hobbies, sports, enemies, holidays, during which they had some sweet tea and biscuits. The family were very helpful but nothing really came from it.

Lisa lowered herself slowly into a hot bath. Below the bubbles she moved her hips in time to the reggae rhythm drifting into the bathroom from the stereo. Her breasts and arms floated and swayed, breaking the white foaming surface. Suddenly, overwhelmed by a rushing sensation, she was sucked upwards into a white void.

She felt vulnerable as she stood, naked, pushing against the soft white webbed walls of the tubular corridor. Bravely she moved to where the tube curved away. It narrowed slightly and fell off in a gentle slope.

"Lisa," a soft female voice called to her. She looked behind to see a naked black woman. "Be careful."

"Who are you?" Lisa asked.

"Please be careful."

"Who are you? Mother?"

Water gushed along the tube; its level was rapidly rising. Neither woman was bothered by the tube filling with water.

"I can't stay," the older woman said and turned away.

"Wait!"

The woman walked in the direction from which

the water flowed then she disappeared into the glowing whiteness of the corridor. Lisa dared not follow.
The water was now at knee height.

"Come back!" she screamed after her. "Who are
you?" The floor beside her began to sag under the
weight of the water and pulled heavily at the walls and
roof section. A split appeared overhead and the blue-
ness of the sky beckoned her. She managed to find
footholds in the webbing but her hands could feel the
fibers coming away as she pulled with the weight of her
body. People peered in from above and reached for
her, offering safety. A red-haired man finally grabbed
her wrist. She felt his enormous power as he easily
pulled her from the fast flowing fountainhead.

The reggae stopped and Lisa sat upright, eyes wide
open. She had had this disturbing dream before.

The murder scene at Parramatta Lake was staked out for
one additional week. Four uniformed men were on
duty, along with either Lisa or Gary. One of them stayed
in the office, sifting through information—telephoning
and later door-knocking. At the lake, they made a sham
of using lots of high-tech equipment with State Police
markings on it; patiently they waited for the killer to
return. He didn't. At least, they didn't see him.

16

After Mr. Chapman was replaced by the blue-haired spinster, Ms. Williams, Bombala became an all-female institution. So, when Lisa had her first period at thirteen, Bombala was void of men. Lisa wasn't traumatized or disgusted at the event, she was simply relieved. Many of her friends already had theirs; it was something of an anticlimax when she awoke early to find she was lying on a red, wet spot.

Lisa had evolved into a shapely young woman. She had lost her pre-pubescent boyish looks and gained well-rounded breasts and hips. Her face had grown longer and her high cheekbones pushed forward. Her wavy brown hair was short, bouncing at the nape of her neck. She loved rock & roll music and she loved it loud.

In the Bombala township a pub engaged bands from Sydney to play in the large beer garden. On Friday and Saturday nights and Sunday afternoons the electronic music could be clearly heard a mile away at Bombala House. That summer, Lisa's favorite pastime was planning various ways which might enable her to go to town to steal a glimpse of the bands. Her favorite plan, the one she returned to again and again, was the one that involved unlocking the dorm door from the inside.

Usually, on Saturday nights, matron called the girls to bed after supper, a shower, a short reading session and one hour of television. She would then switch the lights out and lock the door of the dorm at eight o'clock. The girls had to use poes if nature called through the night. She then retired to her own room which was ten paces along the corridor to watch *Hey, Hey, It's Saturday* on television. It was a source of great amusement among the girls to hear her laugh at the television show. It was not that her laugh was so unusual, as loud—she guffawed like a man.

This particular night, Lisa slipped out of her nightdress. Underneath she was fully clothed. She reached under her pillow for the brown wrapping paper and paddle-pop stick she had taken earlier that day from her craft class. She took her shoes in her hands and silently walked to the door.

"Lisa . . . what are you doing?" one of the girls whispered.

She didn't answer, but kept on her way to the door where she sat on the floor and looked through the large keyhole, trying to gauge where the key was positioned in the chase. Then she started prodding with the wooden paddle-pop stick. The matron always left the key in the door and they often joked about whether she kept them locked safely away from intruders or secured them from the sight of polite society.

Lisa heard the key click as it straightened in the race. She pushed the brown paper under the door beneath the lock then prodded the paddle-pop stick well into the mechanism. On the far side of the door the key fell perfectly onto the brown paper. The girls sat on their beds, giggling and whispering. Lisa carefully pulled the paper back to her side of the door. As she picked the key up her heart pounded so loudly she thought the matron would surely hear it. She opened the door quietly and walked along the corridor to the large double doors at the end. She turned the latch, and then carefully wedged the door closed with a wad of folded brown paper. She drifted into the dark, walking swiftly toward the sound of the loud, rhythmic music.

Matron, of course, was waiting for her at the front door as she arrived back and never, never forgave her.

17

It was late afternoon when Evelyn woke up, surprised to find she had slept most of the day. She peered through the bedroom curtains at the pinkish daylight washing across the western sky. The studio, the classes, she thought—who will take them? It had been the farthest thing from her mind. AIDS, Danny, death and her own mortality dominated all of her thoughts. Her bed sheets were in a twisted coil on the floor at the foot of her bed.

Later that evening she decided to go out and get something to eat and had walked about fifty meters from her home when a well-dressed man in a dark suit with a large nose and long black hair came up to her. He gestured with a cigarette, pushing it forward.

"Do you have a light, please," he said, standing close, smiling, his head angled, looking into her face.

"I'm sorry I haven't. I don't smoke." Evelyn was made uneasy by the glowing, smiling face. She hurried on.

"Wait!" the man called.

Without looking back Evelyn said, "I'm in a hurry,

sorry." She waited to hear if he would follow her, but she heard nothing. She walked quickly and ran when she turned the next corner. Relieved, she pushed the door open to her local café and walked in. She found a table and sat with her back against the wall beneath one of the many framed Toulouse-Lautrec prints that adorned the café walls. The low level light allowed her to lose herself, well camouflaged, in the eclectic mixture of colors in the pseudo-French décor.

"Evelyn, 'ow are you?" Patrice, the owner, asked in his best English.

'*Tres bon monsieur. Et vous*?"

"*Moi aussi*. What may we prepare for you this evening?"

"Something light, Patrice. Let's see," she said, looking at the blackboard to the side of her. "A crepe, yes. The ham and cheese crepe will do just fine, thank you Patrice."

"And a roll and coffee? *Oui*?"

"*Oui, merci*."

He fussed over her, taking a cutlery setting away from the other side of the small, two-seat table. He recomposed everything: the vase containing a solitary silk rose, ashtray, wine glass, napkin. Then he lit the candle.

"No wine this evening?" he asked softly.

"No, mineral water will be fine, thank you Patrice."

"Of course," he said, and was gone.

The man with the unlit cigarette walked purposefully past Café de Patrice to the corner and hailed a passing taxi. The driver abruptly wheeled the cab to the curb causing alarmed drivers behind him to brake suddenly, leaning on their horns as they did so. It was Friday; the traffic was heavy.

"The Marble Bar," he said to the driver. The taxi joined the kinetic stream of vehicles bound for the city.

The Adams Hotel had been demolished to make way for the Hilton Hotel on Pitt Street in Sydney. A provision contained in the development approval for the new building ensured the retention of the celebrated Marble Bar; the bar and décor were finished in the finest Italian marble; the walls boasted numerous original Norman Lindsay oil paintings. Now situated in the basement of the tall international style hotel, the bar was always well patronized on Friday night and considered by both women and men as the best meeting place, the prime pick-up joint in Sydney.

The taxi sped up the driveway to the lobby of the Hilton Hotel. The man with the big nose got out, walked slowly through the lobby and down a set of escalators to the crowded bar. Carefully, he pushed his way through to an empty chair at a table occupied by five young women. "Is this seat taken?" he asked.

"No, it's not," one of the girls said musically, then turned back to her friends. He moved the chair sideways to the table, enabling him to see more of the room. Still standing, he signalled the waitress before finally sitting down.

"How was your meal?" Patrice asked as he expertly cleared Evelyn's table.

"Very good thank you, Patrice."

"And for desert?"

"*Non, merci monsieur,*" she said in an admonishing manner waving a pointed finger at him. "I can't afford the calories."

"What is this you say! You are so beautiful, so slim."

"You Frenchmen know just what to say," she said, and she meant it. "I will have another coffee and more water."

"*Certainement!*"

Patrice had such flair. Evelyn had been eating here for several years and he still managed to make her feel, well, special. He returned to her table with coffee, water and a small silver platter with three chocolates and the bill. A note was wrapped in the bill and Evelyn felt a rush of excitement as she opened it.

Dear Evelyn,

   Please join me for drinks tonight at eleven-thirty when we close the café. The staff and I are celebrating our fifth year in business. Please say you will.
Love,
Patrice.

Patrice stood, watching Evelyn from his maitre d' station near the front door. She smiled and nodded, yes.

The young woman stole a glimpse of the large-nosed man seated next to her as a waitress placed another tall glass of beer in front of him. He wasn't as unattractive as she had first thought.

"It's crowded," she said.

"I like it like that. That's why I come." He had a confident air about him. "You meet lots of interesting people here."

"Have you met any interesting people here?"

"Yes of course."

"Anyone I'd know?"

"Paul McCartney."

"Really!" She turned to face him, smiling in disbelief. "Did he talk to you?"

"Of course he did. He's just an ordinary person like you and me. He talked to a lot of us here that night."

"Who else have you met here?"

"Elton John came in after one of his concerts last year, and Julio Iglesias," he lied, but he knew it was what she wanted to hear. "Elton invited a whole lot of us to a party—the ones who were here at the end of the night."

Contact; they had engaged. He bought her several drinks and soon she hardly noticed his nose. He totally entranced her as he wove his magic of manufactured celebrity about her, charming her with deceit and plying her with alcohol.

"Ally, there's a party on . . . we want to go. Are you coming?" her friend asked. Ally didn't seem to hear her. "Ally!" she called louder.

"Yeah . . . okay, I'm coming," she said reluctantly. The large nosed man looked away, his feelings were hurt. "I'll give you my number," she said.

"No, it's okay, don't bother," he said.

"I want to." She reached into her small handbag and pulled out a pen and paper. "Please call me," she said as she wrote. "What's you name?"

"Peter."

"Peter who?"

"Peter Caulfield." She held his hand and made sure he took the paper with her telephone number.

"Please call me, Peter," Ally said warmly before she, her small group of girlfriends and a handful of young men left, pushing their way through the crowd. She looked across the long room to Peter as she walked up the stairs. Then, at the exit she waved a short, shy wave and left.

Patrice was fidgeting, folding napkins when Evelyn came through the door at eleven-thirty. He rushed to her side and took her by the arm.

"I'm so glad you could join us," he said.

The last two tables of four were on their coffee and liquers. Evelyn could already hear the sound of celebrations in the kitchen. The enchanting sound of rapid and high-spirited French drifted into the dining area. Patrice led her to the kitchen.

"Everyone! Most of you will recognize Evelyn already—one of our very best customers, she has been coming here for many years. Evelyn, this is Robert, my business partner and chef, Marie, Corinne, Michel, Paul, Henri . . . and Barry, the Aussie."

"Poor you," Evelyn laughed. "I hope you can speak French, Barry."

"*Un peu*," he said, indicating a small amount between his index finger and thumb, "but I get by."

"No worry, we will all speak English tonight in your honor," said Patrice, then reached into the refrigerator and took out a magnum of Veuve Clicquot Champagne. Tall fluted glasses were quickly placed in a line on the stainless steel bench.

Evelyn watched Patrice. He was of average height, slim, dark hair with sparkling friendly eyes. He had full pouting Mediterranean lips and a disarming smile. She'd always felt attracted to him. He laughed a lot and made others laugh too with his charming ease. At every opportunity he gently caressed Evelyn. She enjoyed his play.

Twenty minutes later the last customer came to the kitchen to pay his bill and was rewarded with a glass of champagne. Songs sprang from the merry gathering as night transformed to morning.

Ally reappeared. "I couldn't go with them. I didn't like that bunch of guys, they were so immature," she said.

Peter stood up, quickly pulling a chair out for her to sit. "I'm glad you came back."

"So am I." Ally almost missed the edge of the table with her handbag—all the alcohol was affecting her. But she happily drank another two gin fizzes with Peter who, she found much brighter than before.

He launched into more stories of celebrities he had met. Ally listened, mesmerized.

Finally, when he thought the time right, he stood. "Let's get out of here," he whispered.

Ally drained the last drop from her glass and stood also. Then a more serious, intimate air ignited between them as he took her by the arm. Her pulse raced as he led her up the stairs, through the bright lights of the hotel lobby and into a waiting taxi.

Across the city, one mile south of the Marble Bar, Gary sat exhausted; Lisa was spent too, she lay back in her chair, her feet on her desk.

"Come on, let me buy you a drink," Alan Jackson said. They were both startled; neither had heard him walk up to their cubicle.

"Can't refuse the boss," said Gary. "I'm glad some-one can bring an end to this day because I can't."

"Let's go to the Redfern Tavern, it's just around the corner," Jackson explained. He looked nervous. "I'll get my coat."

They followed the senior lawman to his office then out into the coolness of the early morning air. A siren could be heard far off in the distance. Lights flickered, cars screeched and roared.

The Redfern Tavern was officially closed but the police had an arrangement with the licensee: they were permitted to come in via the staff entrance, which was left open. They could have snacks, play pool, listen to music and drink until four in the morning.

There were about twenty uniforms and ten detec-tives, men and women, in the tavern this morning. As the three detectives pushed through the swinging doors, everyone turned and watched them walk to the bar.

"What will you have?" Jackson asked.

"Gin and tonic, lots of ice and a slice of lemon in a tall glass, thanks," Lisa said and smiled. Jackson smiled back. It was worth coming just for that, she thought.

"I'll have a Resch's, thanks," said Gary. There was a pause as the three looked about the room.

"We're not all bigots and racists you know," Jackson blurted out. "Some of us are thinking people with independent, supportive views of Aborigines. You will recall the referendum giving Aboriginal people citizenship rights was won with an eighty percent majority. Well, I'm one of the eighty percent and so are most of my friends." Gary and Lisa were taken aback. As the drinks arrived in front of him, Jackson continued. "I know you haven't exactly been received with open arms here in our department but that's going to change. I've told them. You'll read about it tomorrow in the memo I've sent to all staff. We can't have any divisive bull-shit in our job. It's us against the bastards out there; it's always been that way. And you've joined with us, you're part of our team."

He passed the drinks to each then, turning, he spoke loudly. "Hey everybody, we haven't yet had the usual welcome drink for our new recruits here, Gary and Lisa. So, for the next hour, the drinks are on me or, more correctly, on the department." With that a cheer went up and a scramble to the bar ensued.

Gary and Lisa looked to each other and touched glasses in salute. Jackson noticed; he raised his glass to them. "Welcome," he said loudly. They both knew he really meant it.

Evelyn stood at her front door, took the keys from her bag and handed them to Patrice. He was so quick and so skilful that it seemed like only seconds before she found herself standing in her own hallway with Patrice softly kissing her. She fell slowly back onto the wall as he pressed himself against her, kissing her deeply now. She fell into the well of emotion that had been sealed by the tension of recent events and thoughts of death. She pulled Patrice tightly against her. She wanted to feel life. She was alive! She knew as she kissed him and felt the warmth of his hard body that she desperately needed him tonight.

"I'm not sure about this, Peter," Ally said as they walked along the narrow, dimly lit corridor to his Bondi Beach flat.

"Neither am I," he said as he opened the door. "Let's have a coffee."

"That's a terrific idea," Ally said and flopped down heavily on the lounge. "Woo."

"Are you okay?" he called from the kitchen.

"Yeah, I'm okay now that I've sat down." She looked about the room. "Where's the stereo? Where's the TV?" she asked.

"In the bedroom."

"Can I put some music on?"

"Sure you can."

After he'd placed the kettle on the stove, Peter came into the bedroom to find Ally fussing with the dials of his stereo unit. "Let me," he said. Soft classical guitar music streamed from the speakers. "There." They both stood. He took her by the hand and led her to the bed.

"I can't stay all night," she said softly.

"That's okay." He laid her back on the bed and kissed her. She could feel his excitement mounting. He rolled her on her back and positioned himself between her legs. She hugged him tightly as they kissed. He began writhing, slowly pushing his pelvis against her as he kissed her. The kettle screamed at them from the kitchen.

"Oh shit," she said as he broke away. "Don't go."

"Won't be a minute." Peter ran to the kitchen, switched the stove off, pulled the kettle off the burner, locked the front door and switched off all the lights.

When he came back to the bedroom he found Ally undressed, lying on her back under the covers.

Patrice was such a considerate lover, Evelyn thought, as they lay naked in her wide bed. He began to caress her and kiss her again but more softly now, more slowly, more sure. Neither of them felt hurried—both enjoyed the heightened excitement of a new lover.

Peter excused himself and went to the bathroom. He hastily peeled the false nose from his face and dispensed with the long black wig.

In her intoxicated state, Ally missed him not at all. "You look different," she said as he returned to bed.

"More handsome," he suggested.

"Yes, more handsome."

He pulled the sheets back and took a long look at her nakedness. Finally he spoke. "Do you like playing games, Ally?" His voice shook with excitement. "You know, sex games?"

"Oooh, you lovely erotic man, yes I do. What do you want to play with me?"

"I want to tie you up."

"And then what?"

"You'll see." He took several lengths of soft sash from beneath the bed and began wrapping it around her wrists.

"Kiss me," she said.

"Not yet."

"Kiss me," she insisted.

"Not yet," he said louder. "I'm supposed to be dominating you."

"Is that what you're doing? How exciting." He tied her arms tightly to the bedposts then opened her legs.

"Ooooo." Ally relaxed and smiled. She closed her eyes as he wrapped her ankles and tied each of them in turn to the foot of the bed.

Evelyn basked in the warm afterglow of tender, much needed, lovemaking. Patrice's breathing was deep, slow and regular as he slept beside her. She felt an excitement building in her again, remembering the passion they had just shared. Patrice stirred as she ran her hand over his abdomen. He turned and kissed her gently on the forehead. She was hungry; lifting herself onto one elbow she kissed him passionately. He pulled her tightly against his chest. She felt he was ready for her again, carefully, she moved to straddle him.

"Have you ever seen a gun, Ally?" Peter asked as he produced a small, highly polished handgun. The barrel gleamed in the dim light.

"No, not up close."

Peter showed it to her then positioned himself between her legs and ran the cool steel along her legs from her ankles upwards.

"Oh, Jesus." Ally felt her whole body shudder.

"Does that feel nice?"

"Mmmmm."

"What about, here."

"Uhh, yes." She moved her body, swaying slowly. He lowered himself onto her and kissed her.

"Put it in me, put it in me!" she cried.

He put the barrel of the gun between her legs and rubbed it in time with her movements.

"Not the gun . . . your cock," she insisted while kissing him frantically. His penis found her warm opening. He held the gun tightly beside her ear as he joined her excited rhythm.

"Suck it," Peter said, putting the barrel to Ally's lips. "Come on, suck it." Suddenly she was scared. The steel weapon felt cold against her tongue. She began to shake, quivering with excitement and fear. She could feel his orgasm rising and moaned loudly as her own orgasm was near.

Suddenly, while thrusting frantically, Peter pulled the trigger of the gun: the side of Ally's head fell open, spraying blood, bone and tissue across the bed.

"Oh shit! Oh fuck!" he yelled.

18

Gary looked across the harbor from the busy ferry terminal at Circular Quay as he ate hot chips from a paper bucket. He had been checking records at the nearby Phillip Street police station and arranged for Lisa to pick him up here. It was a crisp summer morning. And he sat, mesmerized, watching the sparkling sunlight on the surface of the water. He wondered what the harbor had been like before 1788 and imagined what life had been like for his ancestors on coastal Australia before the British landed here.

Aboriginal people claim they've always occupied this land and never migrated here, as some academics theorize. They reverse the logic of the popular concept: if people could walk south over the so-called land bridge which joined Australia to Asia, then surely they could also have walked north. After all, the most ancient evidence of human habitation has been found on this continent.

During the sixty thousand years of known human occupation of Australia prior to the first British settlement in 1788, any changes in the appearance of the land were caused by climate. About fifteen thousand years ago, when the most recent ice age was rapidly coming to an end, ice sheets covering the entire southern part of the island-continent (for the second time in one hundred thousand years) were melting and Aboriginal people moved slowly south to reclaim their lands.

When the Malays invaded the Indonesian Archipelago four thousand years ago they got very close but did not quite manage to reach Australia. One thousand years ago the Hindu-Buddhists from southern India began a systematic colonial expansion towards Southeast Asia. This dramatic movement only ceased because of a Muslim invasion of northern India but not before the Indians had colonized land as far south as the islands of Indonesia.

In the early fifteenth century, when Macassar fishing-beds were exhausted, the Macassans sent the Bugis seamen to the north coast of Australia. They named it Marega. The Macassans befriended and traded with the black people they met in Marega. They showed them how to grow and dry certain fruits, nuts and spices, which they themselves would stow and use as provisions for their homeward journey. In return they traded small axes and metal wares. After five hundred years the Macassans had changed the land very little except for a few species of plant foods.

In 1606 the Dutch discovered Australia, the first white people to do so. Captain Willem Jansz sailed his ship *Duyfken* along the west coast of what is now Cape York Peninsula to Cape Keer-weer. One hundred and sixty-four years later Captain James Cook met the Eora people of Marega when he anchored in the bay known as Kamay; he immediately renamed it Botany Bay. In 1788, the British sent their first fleet of colonists, who made camp in Tubowgule, renamed Farm Cove and later Sydney Cove by the Europeans.

One year after British settlement the major source of water for the township, the Tank Stream, had become too polluted to drink.

Gary finished his fried potato snack. Walking past the busy ferry wharfs he made his way across the paved canal, which is the Tank Stream. It still flowed, carrying stinking sewage to the once clear waters of Sydney Harbor. A whole race of people, the Eora, who met Cook here on his historic journey, had been made extinct by the British.

Could humankind ever have experienced more

rapacious development than right here? wondered Gary.

Lisa pulled the police car to the curb and gave three bursts on the car horn. Gary looked up; he was standing in a crowd, watching a painted, clown-like busker, a mime artist, painted half black, half white. He broke away, ran to the car and smiled at Lisa as he climbed in. Lisa accelerated away and they were soon lost in a multicolored sea of moving sedans.

The harlequin opened a small child's school bag and passed it around the gladdened crowd for donations. The people gave generously, then dispersed. The busker picked up his small kit and moved north about two hundred meters then opened his bag again.

An unassuming Aboriginal man took up the original position. He carried a long didgeridoo painted in the elaborate style of the Yirrkala people. He peeled off his shirt and, reaching deep inside a white plastic carry bag, pulled out several small jars of body paint. A family of four American tourists stopped to watch. He applied the paint in long stripes, first to his torso then to his arms, crimson oxide, yellow ochre, white. The crowd swelled to more than twenty. Now he painted his face using deliberate colored dots and concentric circles. The crowd had increased to around fifty. He slowly secured the paint jars, took up his instrument and began to play. The droning music from the hollow log reverberated through the huge number of people listening and watching. He closed his eyes, oblivious to the many banknotes in his large, upturned, cloth cap.

I packed all my things and got out of that room in Bondi as soon as I could. Jesus I was scared. It was the first time I ever killed a white woman. It was an accident. I didn't mean to pull the fucking trigger. I just left her there on the bed and ran to the car, threw everything in the back seat and pissed off as fast as I could.

Lucky I don't have any furniture of my own to lug around. And at all the places I rent I use different names.

I feel okay now because I'm up on the north side of the city in a backpacker place at Collaroy, right opposite the beach. Today, I took all my bloodied clothes and burned them in the large incinerator in the backyard and went for a long walk on the beach. When I got to the shops I bought a hamburger and went around the rocks to eat it. Well, a girl came and set up near me and took all of her clothes off. I mean stark naked! She had a great body, with big tits. I just sat, ate and had a good look. Well, she came and sat next to me. I was there first! When she went in for a swim she put some bikini bottoms on but took them straight off when she came back to our spot. I was disappointed when she left about an hour and a half later. She didn't look at me at all. She pretended I wasn't there.

I wonder what the cops will do now? I'm a bit worried because someone might have seen me leaving those rooms at Bondi. But most of the time I used my disguises. Oh well, I did the best I could; I cleaned everything up and got away as fast as I could.

The whole thing reminded me of the time I scarpered away from home when I was eleven. Dad's mate Alfred had come to stay and the two of them were always drunk. I packed my school bag full of clothes and a couple of toys and ran as fast as I could down the street. I pinched some money out of Mum's handbag so I could get on a bus and go to Mittagong. I don't know why I chose Mittagong; I didn't know anyone there. Then I met good old Joannie, in the park. She said I could stay at her place if I was look- ing for somewhere. She had been shopping and was loaded down with plastic bags. At first I was a bit worried but I thought, why not? It's getting cold and it would be better than sleeping at the railway station which is where I had planned to spend the night.

Joannie's place was only small, made out of tim-
ber. It needed a coat of paint. I guessed it had been
painted light green, once. She was about forty,
slightly overweight and pretty. She lived alone and
drank white wine every night, which she poured from
a flagon into a tall, floral tumbler. That first night
she made us stewed mutton and potatoes and it tasted
great on that cold night. We settled down and
watched television until it got dark. Then she told me
I could sleep in her bed with her, we would be
warmer that way. So . . . I did. It was warmer. She
hugged me tightly and when we were warm and set-
tled she took my hand and placed it between her legs.
She showed me what to do with my fingers so that she
could get off. On other nights she liked it better if we
both were naked but she wouldn't do anything to me
. . . I was the doer. We never really did it . . . you
know, fucked. I stayed with her for two weeks until
the police picked me up in the park one day and took
me back home to Goulburn. I thought there was
something wrong with what Joannie and I were doing
but I didn't mind. I didn't know what exactly was
wrong until years later. Anyway, Joannie was okay;
she was just lonely and horny. She taught me there's
nothing wrong in getting what you want, sexually.

My beach becomes empty when the sun goes down
behind the high ridge behind us. Then the joggers

come out. They come in the early morning too, just after the sun comes up. I would love to jog but my left ankle still isn't better from the time I wrecked it two years ago in Penrith. I fell off my mate's motorbike and they rushed me to hospital. It's never been right. Bastard specialists, you pay them big money to do their job. If I botched up my work the way my doctor did, I'd get the fucking sack.

19

Ally's dead body was found two weeks after her death. Pandemonium washed across the crowded homicide offices at Redfern. Rumors were rife that the Aboriginal rape-murderer might be behind the Bondi killing also. It looked like his signature. More people were assigned—detectives and administrators. The coffee room was converted into a media reception area, with Alan Jackson the obvious choice to address the public.

Police Commissioner Malcolm Patterson, and the State Minister for Police, Terry Meriton, pushed their way toward Jackson's office. They were preceded by sycophantic minders shouting: "Out of the way. Clear the way!" Seven people crowded into Alan Jackson's small office. Yet again he found himself at the center of a hysterical media-driven investigation.

"Sit down Jackson," Patterson said. The seven men looked about them—there were chairs enough for three. Consequently, some remained standing.

The detective staff watched through the large glass panels, which made up the office walls. Thirty pairs of eyes anxiously watched every move, and tried their best to lip-read, hoping to glean information from the executive meeting.

"Just tell me straight Jackson, is it the same maniac who likes to fuck Abo's?" Patterson asked.

Jackson was defensive. "We don't know."

Meriton chimed in. "What is your best guess at this preliminary stage?"

"We don't guess about rape-murders here."

"Don't give me that bullshit! You can save that for those hungry bastards out there," Patterson spat angrily.

"Okay, yes . . . I think it is the same bloke. We're waiting for Forensic to confirm it but we all think it's the same arsehole."

"What else can you tell us?" Patterson asked.

"We believe it was the murderer's flat. It was furnished. The neighbors gave conflicting descriptions of the man who lived there but he is Caucasian, about 175 cm tall, medium weight, dark hair. We have three good sets of fingerprints taken from the flat but none match anything we have, he isn't on our files. He hadn't been living there very long..."

"How long?"

"Eight weeks."

"Who have you assigned the case to?"

"We've got Leslie and Fuller working on it."

"You mean the Abo's—the ones we appointed to look into the black murders?"

"Yes."

"Alan mate, we can't leave those fucking blacks on the case now. Jesus, they're ninety-day wonders. We'd all be out of a job within hours," Patterson spluttered.

"You mean because now the victim is a white woman?" Jackson wanted to hear it stated, have it put clearly so it could go on his statement of record.

"Fucking right! Yes. She's white and you know that's why there are a hundred fucking cameras and microphones in your front office right now. Shit! You tell him, Terry," Patterson said. He sat back in his seat, exasperated.

"It's simple, Alan. We say you've taken the case on personally with a back up of five divisions amounting to one hundred men, eight hundred man hours per day. You understand? That will shut the bastards up for a while. Then in a couple of days, when we have more time . . ." he allowed his thoughts to trail off.

Jackson sat in his chair and took stock. He had heard the media damage-control procedure before. Through the glass windows he could clearly see the dark faces of the two new recruits amongst the numerous white ones. The faces created a wallpaper effect behind the glib politician as he continued to speak.

Twenty minutes later, camera strobe light flashed and brilliant bluish-white television lights had transformed the muster room into a media conference studio. As the police chiefs entered, the sounds of noisy clatter rang out as newsgathering equipment was brought into action. Camera operators pulled focus on Jackson and the two high-ranking officials as they walked to take up their seats at a long table. Drapes hung from wooden battens hastily fixed to the wall behind them. Numerous microphones featuring multicolored media logotypes cluttered the area in front of the police spokespersons. Jackson sat in the middle of the two other men.

"Thank you ladies and gentlemen for waiting patiently," Jackson began. "We've invited you here today so we can accurately inform the people of Sydney about the death of a young woman found late yesterday evening in a rooming house at Bondi." He looked up and scanned the room. "I will read a prepared statement after which I will take questions."

There was a complete silence as Jackson pulled a single sheet of yellow paper from a file folder, then he continued: "At 2:45 A.M. this morning, police were called to premises on Roscoe Street, Bondi where they found the naked body of an unidentified Caucasian female aged between nineteen and twenty-five. She had been raped and brutally murdered. As the head of the Homicide Squad I will take full charge of the investigation and I am informed by the Commissioner and Minister that we may expect five divisions of manpower to assist—that amounts to eight hundred investigative hours per day until this maniac is caught." Jackson had confidently taken charge. "We will now take questions. Please keep them brief. Yes over there." He pointed to a female television journalist he recognized in the surging throng.

"Detective Jackson, can you tell us how the woman was killed?"

"She was shot once in the head through the roof of her mouth." He pointed to another journalist.

"Who found the body?" asked a newspaperman.

"A neighbor complained about the odor. The owner of the building asked us to investigate. The woman had been dead approximately two weeks. Yes, over there." He pointed again.

"Is there more than one person involved here?"

"We are currently only looking for one person."

A question was shouted above the rest. "Is this

murder connected to the Aboriginal murder-rapes in any way?"

Jackson looked quickly in the direction of the Minister then to the Police Commissioner. "Yes. We strongly suspect the crimes were committed by the same person."

"So you're looking for a serial killer?"

Jackson paused then made his admission. "Yes."

The Police Commissioner rose quickly to his feet as numerous questions were screamed across the room, becoming fused in one chaotic chorus. Flashes and clatter rose as an unbearable battlement of noise. "That will be all gentlemen . . . ladies," he said. The din continued as the three men left the room, heads bent.

Gary and Lisa had been asked to prepare a comprehensive file of their findings and pass it on to Jackson. He asked them to stay for a briefing session to which he asked the full complement of detectives.

The muster room was now filled. As Jackson entered, the level of chatter softened. He stood on a chair and took control, fairly shouting as he addressed the detectives. He began by listing details of the long case histories as a ten-page case synopsis was distributed.

"Let's get out of here," Gary whispered to Lisa.

She nodded her approval. They moved along the back wall of the room and left quietly.

"I don't know about you but I feel ripped off," Gary revealed once they were in the street.

"Yeah, I know what you mean. But we're not off the case, we just aren't running it. I'm not going to give them the satisfaction of kicking me out. I'm staying . . . and I aim to use everything, every way I know, to keep my job in the team. Let's force them to notice we're still here."

Gary looked at her. She was determined, angry. He offered her a cigarette as they walked. "You're right," he said. "Let's show those bastards something."

After a first unsuccessful try Gary lit both their cigarettes. Then they faced each other, locked in a gaze, searching the other's face.

"Let's get our trumps out in the open. That Identikit picture, let's get it done and distributed," Lisa suggested. Gary agreed as they moved quickly along the sidewalk with more purpose.

I knew there'd be a fuss about that last one at Bondi; it was too close for comfort. The television news went crazy; I've never seen anything like it. It was as though the reporters were on the side of the cops. It's because she was white. They kicked the Abo cops off the case, although no one is saying so. I feel sorry for them; they're not on TV anymore.

I laughed when I saw the Identikit picture of me in the papers. Geez, you could see it was a false nose, easily. What's wrong with these cops? Maybe I should wear a Groucho Marx mask next then see how they draw me.

Yesterday I went to the beach and sat on the sand all morning. It was hot and all the mothers came down once school had started. Young too, some of them. Mostly they had toddlers with them. I stayed until lunchtime then I went home.

I'm thinking of moving to Queensland. Get away for a while. At any rate, I decided to retire, change, get out of that killing business. Whether I move away or not, I'm going to retire, undefeated.

20

Evelyn sat in Danny Renaldo's office sorting through a pile of letters, which had accumulated in the bright red plastic in-tray. The Girl Friday, Rosie, sat opposite her, they were sharing the charge of the dance company.

Danny had gone to Melbourne for a short stay with friends. Although he felt robust and healthy, he knew the final symptoms of the full-blown AIDS virus; he knew soon he would grow weary and wither. Evelyn had suspected for some time now that he might have tested HIV positive; he had become overly friendly. But she was surprised to learn he had tested positive three years ago. Now he was slowly dying.

Evelyn opened a hand-written letter addressed to Danny. It was postmarked from Richmond, Victoria. She knew as she opened it that it might be personal and it was. She went ahead and read it nevertheless.

Dear Danny,

It has been three weeks since we last saw you although it seems much longer. Please come down and visit us. We miss you. I don't want to be melodramatic about it but you know very well that soon we'll say goodbye for the last time. My last bout of flu left me very weak. I still have some fluid in my lungs.

Ronald is excited about a health camp he heard about which takes in cancer and AIDS sufferers only. The guy who runs it was diagnosed with cancer. He abandoned traditional medicine after chemotherapy left him almost dead. He dropped out; fled to a cave in New Guinea and became a hermit, meditating, dieting, purging. He found, to his own astonishment, that he went into remission. Not only that, his growths actually reduced in size until they disappeared. Eventually he drove the cancer cells from his body completely. Anyway, we are going to try it and we want you to come with us.

If we don't hear from you soon we will phone.

Love, kind wishes and prayers,
Brian and Ronald

Evelyn now suspected she knew where Danny was.

She re-sealed the envelope and put it with the four others she needed to mail to his apartment.

Lisa let the phone on her desk ring at least five times even though she was sitting next to it. Then she lazily reached out and lifted the receiver while still reading a rape-murder debriefing sheet from last year.

"Hello Lisa, there are a couple of teenagers at the front desk for you. They say they're friends of the dead girl found at Bondi." The voice was calm and smug.

"I'll be right there," she said excitedly. Finally their television appeals had come good.

Several minutes later Gary switched an audio machine on to tape an interview of record. He moved his head to speak directly into the microphone. "April 25th, 10.35 A.M. Those present at interview are . . . Detective Gary Leslie, Detective Lisa Fuller, with Elaine and Robyn Murphy. The interview pertains to the Bondi murder of Allison Brompton." At last they knew her name. He paused briefly. "Elaine, tell me what you remember about the night your friend went missing."

"We were all at the Marble Bar early, you know, after work."

"Why didn't you report her missing earlier?" Lisa asked.

"We did, but no one connected it to the murder

until now. She wasn't found right away, was she?" Elaine said.

"Did you all work together?" Gary asked.

"Yeah, we all worked at Mitchell, Lewis, Howell. It's a law firm on Phillip Street. We always went out for drinks on a Friday. It was like an end-of-week celebration. We usually went to the Marble Bar then to a disco or party, or something. Well, that night it was crowded, this fellow comes and sits at the end of our table and chats to Ally."

"Would you be able to identify that man again if you saw him?" Lisa asked.

"Yes, we both got a good look at him."

"Ally said his name was Peter," the older one offered.

Gary and Lisa smiled as they made eye contact.

"We all left and when we got outside the pub Ally said she didn't want to go to the party. She went back to Peter and must have gone home with him."

"Did you see her leave with him?"

"No, but she said she was going to and she didn't go home."

After an exhaustive interview the two eyewitnesses were taken to another police building in central Sydney, where they helped hone the existing Identikit picture to a more reasonable likeness of "Peter."

Three months later, Alan Jackson's massive man-hunt had not progressed at all. Jackson was weary, displaying more anger, more frustration than at any time in his long career. His men had a nickname for the serial killer, "The Black Banger", which over time they simplified to "B-B".

Jackson sat at the bar of the Redfern Tavern in the middle of the night, looking at bubbles rising in his glass of pale ale. The bar was unusually crowded even for a Friday, the large number of police now working at Redfern being the major contributing factor.

Mark Poulos rose from his seat and came towards Gary and Lisa. "Hi Gary, I'm Mark Poulos. Does that name ring a bell?" He paused, watching Gary's response. "Cleveland Street Primary School. Fat little Greek kid."

Recognition finally started to dawn on Gary's face. "Clevo, yes, your father owns a milk bar, right?"

"He *used* to own a milk bar. He's been into real estate for years now."

"Yeah, I remember you. How are you mate?" said Gary as they shook hands.

"Yeah, I suppose my name got punched into your brain so to speak." They both laughed.

"So you're a detective, eh?" Gary smiled.

"Yeah but that's okay. So are you." They joked warmly as Lisa looked on.

"I know the fellas gave you a rough time when you first got here," said Poulos. "Sorry about that. They can be made to change their thinking though. We did it once before at Clevo, right!"

"Right." Gary realized they were excluding Lisa. "Oh look, excuse me. Lisa Fuller, this is Mark Poulos." Lisa and Mark shook hands. "We were old mates at school."

"Hello Mark, pleased to meet you," Lisa said smiling.

"Pleased to meet you, Lisa." said Poulos warmly before turning back to Gary. "Welcome back to the third grade, mate. It's my shout. What will it be?" He looked at their existing drinks on the bar and called to the bartender. "Two beers and . . . is that a gin and tonic?" Lisa nodded. "And a gin and tonic."

Lisa lit another cigarette and leaned back in her seat. "So, Mark, how long have you been in this division?" she asked.

He gave out a huge sigh. "Whew, about four years."

"Where were you before that?" she followed up; she was interested.

"University, I was studying Law but it became too much of a drag. I wanted to get involved in the law, not dabble around the periphery, you know, get right into it."

"So, you became a *cop*," Gary said.

"Yeah, I became a cop."

For the next several hours Gary and Mark talked about old times, happy to have Lisa there to listen and sometimes laugh at the varied versions, faded recollections of their salad days. Lisa found the whole thing amusing; she saw Gary through different eyes. Finally, exhausted, Mark stood and extended an invitation to a barbecue at his house before winter arrived. He'd talk to his wife and set a date. Then he gulped back his remaining half glass of beer and left.

Gary and Lisa sat alone in the corner booth; both were animated and happy. "You wanted the time too," Gary said.

"But it was your idea, you asked me to do it," Lisa laughed.

"Yeah, but you actually went and did it." Gary referred to the one-week holiday they had both been granted. Lisa filed the official requests and confirmation had just come through. Commencing next Monday they had seven days' leave on full pay. They were both feeling jaded about their demotion and wanted time to relax; defuse.

"Alby was delighted. He hardly ever sees me. He

said you see me more than he does." She didn't really want to tell him that. Her face changed, Gary saw it.

"I'll get the drinks," he said, jumping quickly to his feet.

"No . . . I really have to go."

"Don't go." Gary put his hand over hers. "Stay for a while."

She looked at him. "No . . . I really have to go." She rose to her feet and left quickly. Gary watched her walk across the smoke filled room—so did Jackson. He turned, patted the stool next to his and beckoned Gary to join him.

"Is she okay?" Jackson asked as Gary approached.

"Yeah, she's okay." Gary was tired, he gasped as he sat.

"I know it's been tough on you two. We set you up on the stage, threw the spotlight on you, then smack in the middle of your number—we hook you off just when you were beginning to put on a good show. I know how I'd feel. Want a beer?" He didn't wait for an answer; he called to the barman and signalled two with his fingers.

Gary saw this as a chance to get a few things aired. "What really irks us is the way people steer clear of us. Everything we do now seems to bother someone or is an inconvenience to the investigation."

"Like what exactly?"

"Like trying to get time on the main frame computer."

"We have computer operators on that monster who do that for you," retorted Jackson, surprised.

"Yeah, but when we ask for something they want forms to be filled out and signed by you. It's as though they're blocking us out."

"Don't be ridiculous."

"I'm not, I've had a lifetime of that sort of treatment and I know when I've been shown the long way round."

"You're paranoid. You need that bloody holiday," snapped Jackson.

The beers arrived and Jackson paid for them. Gary offered him a cigarette. "Gave them up five years ago. They said I'd be dead within a year if I didn't, emphysema." Gary put the cigarettes back in his pocket. "But don't let me stop you. I loved smoking. I'm not one of those idiot, reformed smokers who preach non-stop, making you feel guilty. Enjoy it, I wish I could."

Lisa drove home slowly. A few early morning workers were on the roads, five o'clock starters; it was now four-forty. Next week she and Alby planned to visit his father at Murrurundi. He lived alone there in a small weatherboard house on the edge of town. His mother had died eight years before from cancer of the cervix. She had never had a pap smear so by the time they correctly diagnosed her it was too far advanced for treatment. Lisa liked Murrurundi but she could only take Alby's crotchety father in small portions; like a well-spiced Tandoori curry. He was one of those men who, when he said the word "fuck" in mixed company, made it sound like the most gross, indecent act, certainly not something lovers should enjoy.

The crisp morning air blew in through a slight opening in the car window, sweeping her hair back from her forehead as she accelerated away from a set of traffic lights.

A blanket of fog sat at the bottom of the valley, almost completely covering the small township of Murrurundi; the trees on the steep slopes surrounding the town were full of color. It was early April—autumn had arrived. Alby had driven the little Ford Laser at the speed limit for the entire four-hour journey so they would reach his father's house by ten o'clock. They managed it with fifteen minutes to spare.

"Oh look, the fog. It looks like a fantasy village," Lisa said softly.

"It will burn off soon."

"I don't want it to burn off."

"But it will anyway. By eleven I reckon." Alby pulled

the car into his father's driveway and honked the horn.

Alby was right, by eleven the fog had disappeared. You could clearly see the town nestled at the foothills of the mountains giving it an enchanting presence. Short, steep hills gave rise to higher hills with clusters of trees rimming the brims. The valleys and flats made excellent horse country and the large studs of the area were world renowned. This was polo country. Australia's richest man had bought most of the surrounding land, and turned much of the district into a private sports arena.

Whenever she could, Lisa ventured onto the dirt roads out of town. Bound for nowhere in particular, she always found breathtaking views. She would take along a picnic pack of meat, cheese, olives, bread, Chablis. Alby usually joined her, but today he had wanted time to be with his father. She hadn't protested. She slowed the car on the narrow road and, looking across the valley, carefully chose a place to stop. High on the hilltop she left the car and walked to the edge of a steep slope; the engine of the Laser was softly humming. From here she could see past the town, along the whole river valley for miles.

She walked back, reached through the car window and turned the motor off—its sound had intruded on the scene. An intense quietness closed in, making her smile.

Two hours later, she lay on a soft, fleecy rug relishing the inner warmth of the moment. The meal was tasty; the Chablis, crisp; the place, serene.

Lisa was fifteen when she took her intermediate certificate exams at Bombala. As she walked from the exam room she knew she had done well, she felt confident. Throughout her ten-year stay she had consistently finished ahead of most of the town school children. Matron elevated the teaching methods at the hostel by boasting as much.

Six months later she packed her few belongings in a well-travelled old suitcase. She was leaving for Cobar that afternoon to begin her life as an adult. The government had arranged employment for her as a domestic for the Dean family on their property; the Deans were third-generation graziers. In her bag she had two envelopes: one a letter of introduction, the other listing her educational and vocational achievements.

Hers was a sad farewell. The usual tears, mostly from the younger girls, reminded Lisa of herself. Why did they cry? she wondered. Did they feel sorry for themselves, or her? The very thought of freedom, such as it might be, exhilarated her. Even a remote grazier's leasehold was better than the government "home" she had known for most of her life.

Lisa was assisted onto the Sydney-bound train by Mrs. Williams. In Sydney she would change platforms and board the all-stops Cobar Mail. Mrs. Williams had never forgiven Lisa her stolen night on the town. Their parting was brief. "Don't talk to anyone," she insisted, then turned on her heel and quickly walked off. The government chains were finally unshackled and Lisa freed. As the train pulled away she almost wet herself with excitement. The realization hit that her plight, her life was now hers to explore at last. Tears fogged the reflected vision of herself in the train window as the rural scenery passed by.

The Cobar Mail was comprised mainly of goods wagons; there were only two passenger carriages at the front of the train. Travelling overnight, it passed through the far northwestern towns of New South Wales, shedding freight cars at scheduled siding stops along the way.

Eighteen hours and many friendly conversations later, despite Mrs. Williams final directive, Lisa arrived at Cobar. She was met by a stern-faced Mr. Dean. He drove the entire twenty miles to his property without saying more than a few words. Lisa didn't mind, she was taking in the countryside: the flat, dry plains did not look as she had expected; to her now they were different, exciting, challenging. She was to live here.

After driving through several gates, across several paddocks and one dry creek bed, they drew up to the Dean farmhouse. It was a large, four-bedroom timber house, square, with a wide veranda on every side. It looked like a big hat with a wide brim. Mrs. Dean and her three children came from the house to greet them.

Mrs. Dean was pretty, Lisa thought and Mr. Dean was more relaxed. She now saw he was younger than she had estimated when she first saw him, and taller, and more prosperous. The arrangement wasn't a bad one, she decided. She knew she didn't have to stay forever, that there would be an end; her contract term was for two years.

Later, after she was shown to her room, Lisa unpacked her things. She put down the two envelopes from Bombala, which she was to give to her employers. She worked carefully at the lip of the sealed flap of the envelope containing her final exam results. Finally it popped open; excitedly she read from it:

BOMBALA HOUSE- EDUCATIONAL ASSESSMENT

To Whom It May Concern
    This letter is to inform the reader that at the time of discharge from this facility Lisa Chatfield was examined and found to be illiterate. Despite

*our best efforts, Lisa, like so many of her race, is
unable to learn.*

*She has been in the care of the Bombala Home
for eleven years during which time she has shown
that she can be an obedient worker. We have
drilled her well for work as a domestic.*

*Should you require further information con-
cerning our former charge please don't hesitate to
write to me personally.*
Yours faithfully,

*Mrs. M. Williams. Matron – Bombala
Home for Girls.*

Matron's vindictiveness had followed her to Cobar.

Lisa later pretended to have lost the letter. She
asked Mrs. Dean if she would write away for her
Intermediate Certificate. She did happily. A few
weeks later, Lisa was proud to show the Deans her
true ability as measured by the State exam: she had
achieved better than 90 percent in all subjects.

Over the following months, when shopping in the
town, Lisa was reviled at how Aboriginal people now
lived on the fringe of white man's society: degraded,
void of culture and pride. But the Dean's were a
kind, Christian family. Lisa developed a strong
bond with the children.

Mr. Dean conscientiously sent Lisa's pay to the government trust fund set up for Aboriginal youths for their future security as the contract required, but she never received any payment. Neither did most Aboriginal children similarly forced into organized enslavement.

"What do you reckon, we eat out tonight?" Gary startled his wife, Helen. She looked up from the television screen with wide eyes.

"That'd be great," she said. The current affairs program she was watching did not compete with dining out. "Where do you want to go?"

"How about Italian? I feel like Italian."

"You're on, mate, let's go." She tossed a cushion from the couch at Gary's head. He ducked.

She thought back to the last time she had him to herself for an evening—it had been almost a year ago, when he was studying at the academy. She called the babysitter. Nowadays, on the rare occasions Gary came home early he would be withdrawn, read or study files from work. Helen really looked forward to their time together for the next week.

Helen was slim, with a deceptive appearance of being tall: she was five feet seven. Her long blonde hair fell onto her shoulders. She had small, shapely breasts, the body of an Olympic track athlete. Her deep tan gave her a glowing healthy radiance and when she smiled she could disarm both women and men. She stepped from the shower and toweled down in the bedroom. Gary looked on.

"God, you're beautiful," he said. Reaching out he pulled her to him. She gasped, her wet hair brushed against his face as he kissed her. They fell onto the bed.

"The restaurant?" she whispered. "The Italian— David may not be asleep yet." His kisses prevented her from saying more.

As they entered Fioretti's, the maitre d' smiled from his station beside the lectern near the door and marked an oversized tick beside their name in the diary. The unmistakable aroma of Mediterranean culinary blends wafted from the kitchen, filling the popular inner-city dining spot. The restaurant was divided into three large rooms. The décor was very Italian: white stucco walls, large terracotta floor tiles, red and white checked cotton tablecloths, lots of baskets, red pots and vases. They were seated in a corner of the middle room.

"This is the table reserved for lovers," the waiter said. That's us, Helen thought, remembering the beginning of the evening. The waiter left menus and promised to return soon.

"He's nice," Helen said. "I like the way Latins give special attention to love and lovers."

"When all the while he's thinking of the many ways he would like to devour you," Gary cracked.

"He made that obvious when he first looked at us."

"Looked at you," Gary corrected her.

"Well yes, I don't think he was really too interested in you, dear."

Exotic whiffs from the antipasto sideboard reached them. "Mmmmm, that's a wonderful collection of smells. They do it on purpose don't they?" Helen smiled as she raised her nose to the air.

"Yes they do. Let's get some of it here real quick," Gary said, concentrating on his menu.

"With a good bottle of full-bodied red."

"And some hot rolls," Gary added. He half stood and waved his menu to get the waiter's attention. The poor fellow fairly ran to their table when, for the first time, he took in Helen's smile.

21

Evelyn had an aversion to flying, but when the opportunity came for her to visit her friends, the Johnsons, for half the normal fare, she had to go. She hadn't seen them for almost a year. They frequently wrote and spoke on the phone but it was never satisfactory.

Christine Johnson had been very generous to Evelyn in her student days and she liked to visit her when she could. Christine was a choreographer; she had booked gigs for Evelyn when she was only sixteen, mostly pub gigs. Evelyn was under the legal age then, for performing in premises where liquor was being served. You had to be eighteen in the State of New South Wales. Christine risked it and booked her anyway—she looked older. Then, in the space of one week, nearly all the pubs went topless. Christine tried to find venues where Evelyn wouldn't have to bare her breasts but it became increasingly difficult. Finally, Evelyn told Christine she didn't mind dancing without a top. She was under no illusions about her body; her boobs were not what you would call huge, she was sure they would not cause any riots in Sydney's noisy pubs. A lot of friends from her dance class were doing it, so why the big fuss? After her first topless gig they were both relieved. The work rolled in and the money gave Evelyn a sense of security for the first time in her life.

Christine's husband, Paul, was a kind man. A quiet type, he was a former writer of television plays for the BBC at Pebble Mill in Birmingham. He never did fit in, in Australia; his ingrained, impervious British reserve impeded that.

The jet aircraft banked gently. As the wings dipped, Evelyn saw the small Maroochydore airport below.

Christine was waiting at the baggage checkout area; she waved and called to Evelyn as she approached. They chatted excitedly on the long drive back to their house, which was situated away from the coast, high on the plateau hinterlands overlooking a river. Paul met them at the gate. He had prepared an elaborate luncheon on the large deck overlooking an inspiring sylvan setting stretching to the faraway hills. The ocean was visible in the distance.

"We have the most wonderful market here at Eumundi," Christine said as they sat and began their lunch. "It's on every Saturday. Afterwards we always go to a terrific pub directly opposite for drinks and dinner. They brew their own beer on the premises, Eumundi Bitter. It's the best pub on the Sunshine Coast. I'm sure you'll like it."

"I'm sure I will. It sounds lovely," Evelyn said, relaxing now that her airborne ordeal was over. Noosa promised her quiet, remote, seclusion.

The first day the weather turned cold I just left for Queensland. I went on a bus—it only took fourteen hours to get to Surfer's Paradise.

It wasn't much warmer there than Sydney really but I put up with it. The whole place is like Kings Cross and Disneyland rolled up in one. It's lit up at night like a disco, or circus. But geez, I hate it when people come up to you on the street and want to sell you things or try to make you go somewhere you've never heard of—they're at you all the time up there. But the women, they're everywhere.

I've got a theory about women; they go away on holiday where no one knows them so they can play up, root around, and you know, who cares. Not them. They are ready and ripe here but when they get back home it's a different story. So, once a year it's "let's go sex crazy". They are young too, most of them teenagers.

I remember when I was a teenager, just after I turned thirteen I was about to take a bath. The water was still running and I stood there naked waiting, feeling my cock. By the time the tub was full it was as hard as a rock. I loved the privacy of the bathroom . . . you know, for having a pull. Only this day I kept hearing Mum come up to the door and then go away. A little later my Dad came up and knocked. He said something like: "What are you doing in there, mate? Hurry and come out." I just kept on playing with myself, it felt real stiff. He came back with Mum and both of them were at me. "Come out," they said. Finally he broke the door in. "We know what you were doing," my Mum said. "We're not stupid." From that time on until years afterwards, I had to take my bath with the door open. My mother sometimes even sat on a chair next to me while I had a shower or bath. I should have gone into their bedroom and sat next to them when I heard them fucking. See how they liked that. But all of that was nothing compared to my dad's drunken friend Alfred, the poofter, who fucked me up the arse every chance he got from when I was seven years old.

I left Surfer's Paradise after only a week; it was too cold and too expensive. I ended up at Noosa Beach on the Sunshine Coast. When I raided Evelyn's garbage, I found a letter, from a friend of hers; I knew she would go to Noosa sooner or later, so I came up first. The town was smaller and better up there. I got a part-time job at a small seafood restaurant right beside the river. I worked as a

*kitchen-hand, washing dishes mostly. After a few
weeks I started to wait on tables, I liked it then. You
get to meet people and you can crack onto girls real
easy; girls who are on holiday where no one knows
them, ready for their yearly, sex-crazed week or two.*

*The best one I met was a local girl, Colleen; she
had long, red, wavy hair, was a little overweight but
she had these big tits. She looked great! She used to
sell cotton knitted sweaters at the Eumundi market.
She knitted them herself; they were Australian tourist
type things. I sat there on Saturday mornings with
her. Then afterwards all the people who had stalls
would go to the great old pub across the road. They
made their own beer there, right in the pub. I liked it.
A lot of black girls started coming into the pub and
geez, they looked good. I got turned on as soon as they
walked in. It got that way that every Saturday night I
would be waiting for them to come in; I always felt
much better when they did. Colleen was awake to me,
I think; because afterwards I would make her wear an
Abo T-shirt to bed then I'd fuck her brains out.*

In the calm, stillness of night, Alby rolled on his side
and reached across the bed for Lisa. She woke to the
warmth of his touch. He pulled himself closer.
"Don't Alby. He can hear us," she whispered. He
rolled away from her onto his back and let out a huge

sigh. He knew she was right; his father was old but he wasn't deaf and the thin walls in the old house were definitely not soundproof. For weeks now she had avoided his advances. But he let the matter drop until they were home. He would not feign happiness though; Lisa would feel his displeasure later.

The following morning Lisa rose early. Alby grunted and snorted as she moved. Quietly she dressed and walked the short distance to the town shops for newspapers, freshly baked rolls and fruit. It was cold; the air was still, the remaining leaves on the trees had turned red, gold and brown. Lisa had once thought of buying a house in Murrurundi, she loved it so much. If it weren't for Alby's father living in the same town she would have considered it more seriously. Alby's father and Lisa had an understanding: they didn't like each other and that was that. She could not really enjoy living here, with him nearby, so she filed the idea at the back of her mind. He was becoming more frail each year and wouldn't live forever. Alby would get his house and she could help him renovate—she filed it all away.

Lisa walked slowly back to the house, occasionally stealing a glance at the newspaper. As she drew closer she could see Alby in the front garden working with a heavy mattock and fork. She smiled; she hadn't known him to take any interest in gardening. She was the earth person, the conservator, the nurturer. He was the building person, the scientist, the engineer. Their friends said that between them they had the most wonderful dichotomy of philosophies, the perfect guests for interesting dinner party debates.

The smell of broken earth brought forward the warmth of a deeply held, psychological notion, which Lisa secreted away. Maybe it dwelled in a stream of spirits, or perhaps an imprint of a former self, a peasant, a farmer, an Aboriginal gatherer?

"I love to see you working the soil," she called ahead to Alby.

"Yeah, women enjoy seeing their men sweat, I've been told."

"No, I really think it has more to do with role reversal. I'm the one who nests, remember?"

"Don't give me that shit. What about the pot plants? Who insisted on getting those? Who looks after them?"

"Me."

"You do not!" Again, his feelings were hurt. He stopped working and looked her directly in the eye. "You know I do."

"Sure," she said, walking by him with a smile, which he interpreted as a smirk.

"Hey, wait a minute."

"I've got hot bread for breakfast, got to get inside."

Alby stood for several seconds and watched her walk into the house; his mouth had fallen open. She really was beautiful; he loved her style, her poise, he was becoming aroused. He would have to put off being the injured party because of no sex. He would see if he could talk her into going home early. He thought, maybe she would agree to go home, back to Sydney, tonight.

Lisa opened the bed-covers revealing her naked body. Alby's eyes focussed firstly on her breasts, then he slowly scanned her body stopping at the softness of her pubic hair. They had arrived home just before dark and were in bed ten minutes later. Half of the remaining week's holiday was spent in bed, making love, trying to make up for recent lost opportunities.

Alan Jackson fell heavily against the door of the toilet in his Penrith home, deeply gashing his forehead; blood flowed freely from above his left eye. The intense pain in his chest and left arm caused him to empty his lungs, he could not regain his breath. All light faded; his eyes closed, behind his lids the color red turned to blue before everything fell into blackness.

Within fifteen minutes of his wife calling the ambu-lance, they had him in the intensive care ward of the local public hospital. The following day panic set in at Homicide Headquarters.

22

Gary was driving, but his car knew the route better than he. It moved through the tightly packed scrum of sedans speeding towards the Manhattan-like skyline. It annoyed the red Ford Falcon, which had to brake to make way for it. Cleverly it crossed into the fast lane, eager to get beside a small Bavarian sports job transporting a flaxen-haired female wearing a stern face and men's clothing. Totally without Gary's permission, the car challenged the amber light, and lost; running the red near the football stadium, it sprinted over the rise out of the way of cross-flowing traffic. It blasted angrily on its horn—*pedestrians!* It slowed noticeably near Redfern. Gary was startled, genuinely surprised he had reached the office—he remembered very little of the journey.

Lisa had a coffee ready for him on his desk. She was on her second cigarette. "Can you believe it? He's come in." She raised her eyebrows nodding in the direction of Jackson's office. "He called an urgent meeting for this morning."

Through the heavy glass panels of his office, Gary looked at the tired, grey-skinned leader as he pored over tall towers of paper. He was spinning back and forth, clutching forms and memoranda between his thick fingers, moving them from one stack to the next. He would take a brief glance, sign his name or scrawl instructions before placing them on another tower.

Jackson was back on the job. It was seven-thirty, Monday morning—three days after his heart attack. The staff gathered in the muster room.

"I'm not here to fuck around with you blokes," he called as he crossed the large room. "We are in deep shit. More correctly, I'm in deep shit. This fucking job is not going to put me into an early grave." Jackson was angry; he paused. "I really need your help," he was forced to stop, charged with emotion. Tears flooded his narrowing eyes. "I can't get past this by myself . . ." He could not continue.

There was a long pause, then a collection of whispers whiffed about the room. Suddenly, Gary shouted, "It's okay Alan; we know what's needed mate. Go home and leave it to us."

The hearts of the hardened detectives yielded. "Yeah, go home!" they called in chorus. "Go home!"

Jackson was buoyed, inspired by the spirit of his workmates. He slowly left the room amid cheers and clapping, providing a rare moment for all those present. It was something they would always remember.

Danny Renaldo had lost forty kilos. His cheeks were hollowed, his skin pale yellow. Around his sunken eyes, large brown rings had formed. His hair had thinned and turned grey. He sat with eighteen others in the lotus position on a very large Afghan rug. Through floor-to-ceiling windows he could look onto the green, pastoral scene of the Otway ranges. He listened to the calming tones of self-healing Guru, Lew Cawley. "If you are having trouble getting into it, you really should come back for the next session in a couple of hours time. Don't force the issue. You will only generate frustration." He paused briefly. "If you aren't moving into the meditative state after a few minutes, stop! You will only turn what should be a relaxing, healing moment into an unwanted stressful event, producing the opposite result. Now, some of you may want to leave the room. We will wait, please don't hurry."

Seven years before, Lew Cawley had two growths larger than tennis balls on his left lung. He studied meditative techniques, stuck to a no-fat diet, lived the life of a cave-dwelling hermit and clung desperately to hope. He claimed to have won. His tumors dramatically reduced in size and eventually completely disappeared, leaving him totally healed. He insisted it was no miracle. Now he passed his techniques and methods onto others.

Danny decided to join three others from the group who were quietly leaving the room.

Cawley continued. "Shall we begin?"

A collective reply came from the group.

"I want you to feel that positive expectation, the one you take with you to the theater when you really want to enjoy yourself." The Guru continued, "That's the attitude to bring to meditation. Relax . . . let it happen. Let it wash over you. The more you try to take control, the more difficult a barrier you will construct." His voice trailed off.

Danny wheezed; breathing was difficult. The pain in the center of his back was like a bad cramp that would not relent. He sat cross-legged, feeling his chest muscles straining, bringing him air. He had no more strength with which to fight. If death was near, so be it, he no longer cared. It was more important to him to relax his chest muscles. To his mind, if the reaper appeared soon, he would graciously accept his mercy and peace.

From the air, the long thin strip of parkland designated as a marketplace in Eumundi, Queensland, looked like a swarming ants nest. The ants were organized in an orderly fashion, politely pausing to pass each other on narrow, well-trodden walkways and feasting on large crystals of colored sugar.

Closer up, late-arriving cars slowly cruised the road looking for non-existent parking spaces. Eventually the occupants drove away, resigning themselves to a long walk. The nearest parking space this particular Saturday morning was a kilometer away.

Since Evelyn was still asleep, Christine and Paul took breakfast without her in their sun-drenched dining room. The two-story cedar and glass home was so filled with plants that it was difficult to see where interior met exterior. Tall windows ran the whole perimeter of the house. Numerous doors, which led onto spacious decks, were open. A stairwell filled with tropical trees and shrubs was its focus, over it a glass pyramid allowed natural light to spill into the center of the home.

Eventually Evelyn emerged and ventured down the stairwell to find the house empty. Paul was occupied on a project in the backyard, cutting a pathway through the dense growth to the fast flowing creek below where he planned to build a teahouse. Christine was busily netting leaves and moths from the swimming pool.

Evelyn walked out onto the deck, relaxed, well-slept and stretching luxuriantly. "Hello," she called to Christine, waving her arm in a wide arc. Christine looked up, smiled and waved back.

Christine served Evelyn coffee with fruit and nut bread she had baked that morning. Over the cups, they sat on the deck and talked animatedly. When Paul joined them twenty-five minutes later, they decided to swim, shower and take in the local market.

The number of people attending the market had grown substantially throughout the morning, the three friends had to walk a kilometer and a half from their car to the beginning of the market stalls. People gently pushed, moved, swarmed, pressed and laughed good-naturedly; a contagious, gala atmosphere prevailed.

"If we get separated let's meet underneath that Jacaranda tree in half an hour," said Christine, pointing to the tree with its shock of glowing blue blossoms. Then eagerly, they joined the slow moving, browsing mass of bargain hunters.

I couldn't believe my fucking eyes when she pushed her way along the path. Evelyn, my fucking delicious Evelyn, right here at our markets. I knew she was coming but you have to admit fate had a hand in this. It was meant to be. You know I really tried to retire. I moved interstate to get away. I knew if I kept it up, the killing, I would get caught sooner or later. If Evelyn showed up well, that would change everything. I've been worried about getting caught, especially after that white sheila. Geez, that really put the wind up me. It was an accident though. I hadn't killed any white sheilas before. I suppose I was lucky that I chose blacks. There really isn't as much fuss kicked up about them, is there?

Evelyn walked up to Colleen and me. She liked the sweaters. When she picked one up I jumped to my feet and asked if I could help. She looked at me and, at first, I thought she recognized me. Colleen went red. Evelyn smiled and said she was only looking. She looked at a few more then she walked away. I watched her arse as she wandered along slowly with the crowd, geez.

I saw her go out of sight and waited for a few minutes. Then I told Colleen I wanted a drink, that I'd be back in a minute. I went off in the other direction and doubled back. I soon found Evelyn and a good-looking older woman stopped at a pen stall. She was really interested in the pens; they were imbedded in stems of tree branches. She tossed her head back and let out with a laugh. Turning sideways she saw me watching her.

Evelyn felt disturbed by the man staring at her in the market. He looked really familiar. Then she remembered; he was the one at the sweater stall. He did pay her some attention but she dealt with him politely, she thought. She was certain she had seen him before today, maybe in Sydney.

He disappeared into the crowd. Evelyn wondered if she was being paranoid, but something about him was disturbing.

Later that evening in the Eumundi hotel, Evelyn was swept up in the party atmosphere; she was having a wonderful time. They had consumed a simple pub dinner of scotch fillet steak, potatoes, salad, a roll and red wine. Paul was such a lush, she thought, smiling, a polite friendly lush, but a lush nevertheless. He came out of his shell after a few drinks. He danced with them both and sang along with the blaring jukebox—Beatles, Rolling Stones, Dylan. He was a very enjoyable drunk.

"Jesus, it's great to see you again, I've missed you," Chris said. "You should move up here."

"Oh sure," Evelyn laughed. "What on earth would I do up here?"

"Get into arts and crafts."

"No thank you, not just yet."

"What do you mean by, *not just yet?*"

They both laughed out loud. Then across the room, Evelyn saw him again: the man from the market. He smiled at her and tilted his head back and glowed. She *had* seen him before! That tilted, glowing head? He was the man who asked her for a light for his cigarette! He looked slightly different but she had no doubt—it was him. His face glowed like that of a born-again Christian. As if he had just discovered the meaning of life. He kept staring, amused. Evelyn felt uncomfortable; she turned back to the table, her mood completely changed.

"Don't look now Chris, but there's a creepy guy over there smiling at me. I remember him from Sydney. He tried to pick me up. It was at night, on a deserted street. He scared me."

Paul was singing, engrossed in a Beatles song, oblivious to their conversation.

"Where?" Christine asked.

"Near the big plant on the balcony. Don't look!"

"What do you want to do?" Christine said, her face abstractly vacant.

"Let's leave."

Christine took hold of Paul's arm, signalling to him that she and Evelyn were ready to leave. He looked disappointed at first but after a short exchange, nodded, stood up and continued singing as they walked a zigzag path through the closely gathered tables.

The man on the balcony downed his drink,

grabbed his girlfriend's arm and after a brief conversation they too disappeared into the night.

"What's going on?" Paul said, straightening up as
they pulled out of the car park.

Evelyn confessed. "I think I spotted a creep who
tried to pick me up once in Sydney. I saw him in the
market today then again at the pub tonight. He keeps
smiling at me. I can't explain it. He's weird."

When Christine pulled the car into the driveway
of her home she doused the headlights. She looked
frantically behind them.

"What is it?" Paul asked.

"He's followed," Christine answered. "It's okay,
let's walk calmly into the house and call the police."

They went into the house. Without putting on
any lights Paul managed to find the phone and dial
the police.

A car slowly rolled onto the end of their driveway,
flashed its headlights off, then on, then off, and on
again. The driver's side window was lowered: a male
voice called from the open window.

"Evelyn!"

Evelyn was stunned that he knew her name. She
started to tremble and sank to the floor confused.

"Evelyn!" he called again musically; obviously he
was very drunk. Then with a screech of wheels he

reversed the car from the driveway and the old V8 roared as it sped away.

The three friends huddled together in the darkened house and waited for the police.

Lisa read the message on the yellow Postit which was stuck on the screen of her computer: call *Doctor Nick Kanoulanos (070) 532 174*. There was no mention of what the doctor wanted to ring her about. She dialled the interstate number.

"Hello, could I speak to Doctor Kanoulanos please? Yes, I'll hold . . . Detective Lisa Fuller from the Homicide Squad in Sydney."

It was obvious the receptionist had been warned she might call; she put Lisa through immediately.

"Hello, I'm so glad you could get back to me so soon." He spoke quickly, using crisp staccato syllables.

"Part of my training doctor, how may I help you?"

"I think it is I who may provide you with some help." He laughed at his own attempt at levity, and then continued. "It's in connection with the murders of Aboriginal women. Late last year I treated a young Aboriginal woman from this community."

"Exactly what community is that, doctor?" Lisa asked as she scribbled notes onto a foolscap pad.

"Weipa, on the far northwestern Queensland

coast—we're on the opposite side of Cape York Peninsula to Cairns. The woman's name is Alice Meriga. Her parents brought her into the surgery and she had the most horrific head injury. She'd been raped by a white man then shot in the head and left, presumed dead. She was living in Sydney at the time but refused to go to hospital and her parents arranged for someone to fly her home. It's a miracle she's alive to tell the tale."

Lisa's back stiffened and a warmth ran through her body. A surviving eyewitness! We're back on your trail you bastard, she thought.

"We're onto you," she whispered.

"What was that? What did you say?"

"Nothing doctor. Is Alice still in Weipa?"

"No, she's visiting family near here but will be back tomorrow."

"Good! That's excellent! Please, can you make sure she stays there? We are on our way up. And thank you . . . thank you very much for calling me."

Gary was bent on one knee at a filing cabinet as Lisa let out a Rebel Yell. He broke into a smile and hurried to her, wanting to hear the reason for the outburst.

The small aircraft was filled to capacity. Of the twelve passengers on board eight were dark-skinned people from Weipa: Jirjorond people. In contrast, the white people seemed very white. A friendly white couple told Gary that they were moving to Weipa to start a new life. The husband had got a job in the new bakery there. His wife was looking forward to enjoying her very young baby. John, a local Jirjorond, explained his job as a tourist guide to Lisa. He took tourists into the bush and showed them Aboriginal survival techniques, including bush-tucker hunting and gathering.

Lisa had some inkling of what to expect at Weipa. She had heard about crocodiles, heat, humidity and of course the overwhelming presence of the multi-national bauxite mining company. None of those vague pieces of information seemed relevant as the small aircraft circled the unsealed landing strip below.

As the aircraft banked to align itself with the end of the runway, fires could be seen smoldering to the south of the airstrip. Lisa wondered if they were lit as part of a traditional Aboriginal regeneration burn off. The incredible foliage fairly forced its way through the light blue smoke and cut a striking edge against the warm, greenish waters of the Gulf of Carpentaria.

Albatross Bay was directly below. Lisa could see the historic Duyfken Point, which the Dutchman

Willem Janz named after his ship. He'd made camp there a hundred and sixty-four years before the British "discovered" Australia.

The plane dropped quickly, falling heavily onto the red gravel runway. The terminal consisted of an open canopy, like a large carport with a small garden around its perimeter. Weipa village lay straight ahead. The small community was home to about five hundred people.

As Lisa and Gary retrieved their luggage from the plane, a young black man came up to them and introduced himself in a mumbled voice. He started by calling himself Marcus, then changed it to Michael, then quickly to Mitchell. Lisa and Gary were a little bemused, but found out later that relatives named Marcus and Michael had recently died, so tradition dictated, out of respect, he assume another name for a reasonable period of mourning.

Mitchell said he would drive them to the doctor's surgery. An arresting scent of tropical blossoms hung in the air as they passed a row of houses, the football oval, around a copse of tropical trees and up to a small collection of officious looking buildings. He announced their arrival by honking the horn of the four-wheel-drive diesel utility as the car slid to a stop on the loose gravel. No one looked in their direction; they were used to Mitchell's auto antics.

Music from the community canteen drifted over the playing fields as a local band tuned up. Mitchell explained that a small celebration for the local football team was planned for that evening: a fundraiser to get the team off to a good start in their quest to win the annual knockout competition in Cairns.

Doctor Kanoulanos came from his rooms and greeted the travel-weary detectives. "Welcome to Weipa. Call me Nick," he said cheerily. He was tall and black-haired with wide, striking gray slashes at the temples. His blue, open-neck, cambric shirt allowed an over abundance of chest hair to spill out. The blue Levis hugged his buttocks, clearly defining their shape. They were pulled up tightly around his ample genitalia. Doctor Nick was born in Greece and had come to live in Australia with his parents in the fifties. He did almost all his schooling here.

"Thanks," said Gary. "I'm Gary Leslie and this is my partner, Lisa Fuller." They shook hands and smiled as the doctor ushered them through the door.

"Come, let's go to my office, it's air-conditioned."

A unified gasp of relief was the only reply.

They walked through the waiting room, which was cluttered with paraphernalia, stacks of magazines, journals, toys and newspapers. Red dust was on everything. The actual surgery was a little better:

more organized piles. Nick pulled out two chairs for his visitors.

"I've organized accommodation for you both at the house of the local schoolteacher, Marie Stephens. We only have one small school here, you see. You know the old one-room concept. Marie teaches all grades."

"That sounds great doctor, thank you," said Lisa as she sat.

"Please call me Nick," he insisted.

"Okay." Lisa smiled; she liked him.

"I'll take you to meet Marie shortly," he said after they had talked a while.

"And Alice?" Gary said, quick and to the point.

"Yes . . . and Alice, of course. She is expecting you."

"It has been a long trip. We started at seven this morning." Lisa tried to maintain a friendly atmosphere.

"Well, what is it now? . . . Four . . . so it *has* been a long day for you hasn't it?" he smiled directly into her eyes. "Can I offer you a cool drink?" the doctor asked.

Doctor, you're flirting, Lisa thought. She didn't mind.

"I wouldn't say no," Lisa laughed and Gary joined in.

23

Danny Renaldo sat in a wheelchair beside Jean, a female aide from the Self-healing Health Farm. Danny was less talkative these days but that didn't deter Jean, she did all the talking.

Jean was a big woman in her early forties with very large breasts. Her straight brown hair was cut short in a pageboy style. She wore pants and a sweater. No uniforms were permitted at the farm; they tried to minimize the impression that they were a clinic, a hospital.

"I think we should stay and watch the sun go down. What do you think, Danny?" Jean asked, tilting her head to look him in the eye. There was no reply so she decided for him. "Yes, well I think we should."

Danny felt the despair of loneliness. He had broken off all contact with his family when he first learned he was HIV positive. His parents had divorced. He lost contact with his father (he went off with a younger woman) but his mother had always written every two weeks or so and he to her, although sometimes he would only write a card. When his diagnosis came through he decided to return her letters, marked "not at this address", wanting to spare her.

The white-bright sun became an orange sphere before falling from view below the mountains. Danny Renaldo slumped forward in his wheelchair, dead. He was twenty-four years old.

The tropical heat and humidity was stifling as Gary, Lisa and Doctor Nick strolled along the red dirt road.

Dressed only in shorts and wearing no shoes, children ran out to meet the newcomers. "Not now. But come over to the canteen tonight, okay?" the doctor said good-naturedly. ". . . okay?" The children left, placated.

He turned back to Gary and Lisa. "There's a celebration in our canteen tonight after which I've arranged a barramundi barbecue for you. By then it'll be a lot cooler." He felt relaxed now. He let out a huge sigh of relief after maintaining his composure for so long. "Gary, you and I can go swimming later," he said, feigning a manly punch at Gary's upper arm.

"Sounds great. I'll take you up on that," Gary

said. He meant it; he wasn't being polite. Lisa looked up.

"I'm sorry, Lisa. The men all go to a particular spot reserved for them alone. I'm sure there's a place where women go to swim but I honestly don't know where that is. It's forbidden for men to know. I know the women head south."

All of the houses in the small community were built from Besa-bricks, a cheap concrete compound. They had sheet-metal roofing. None had seen a coat of paint in a decade. The houses were really only used at night to sleep in. People here still preferred to cook, eat and live in the open air. They had their favorite shade trees where they congregated during daylight hours. They walked past a large group of women being very vocal and animated, seated under one such tree—a card game was in progress. Finally they slowed as they reached a house, which was partially covered by vines. The three-bedroom bungalow was set back amongst a cluster of short tropical shrubs with taller trees in the backyard.

"Here we are," Nick said. He called in the direction of the house. "Hello in there, it's me. Doctor Nick."

A middle-aged man and woman sat on the veranda. They stood, looked briefly at the strangers, smiled, and then diverted their eyes shyly to the ground.

"Hello Luke . . . Mary. These are the people I told you about. They've come up from Sydney to talk to Alice. This is Gary and this lady is Lisa."

Gary nodded and smiled.

"Hello. How are you?" Lisa said warmly. "It's hot up here isn't it?"

"Yeah, it can get pretty hot here," Luke responded. There was a brief pause then he laughed nervously.

"Is Alice there?" Nick wanted to know.

"Yes, she's here. Alice!" Mary called. A distressed look swept over her face as her only daughter walked around the corner of the house.

Several minutes later, Lisa had skillfully arranged a private interview for Gary and herself with Alice. As they sat on the ground under a shade tree near the house they explained they were trying to find her attacker and desperately needed her help. Alice sat with her hands tightly clasped in her lap. She had long, wavy brown hair falling to her shoulders, dark brown skin, a pointed nose, and a long oval face with white teeth that sparkled when she smiled.

Lisa pulled a tape recorder from her bag, switched it on and set a microphone in front of them. "Alice I know it won't be pleasant for you but please cast your mind back to when that man attacked you," Lisa said softly.

"He was an ordinary sort of a man . . ." Alice started, but she paused, distressed.

"Just tell it from the beginning, like a story . . . step by step until you get to the end," Gary said gently.

Alice took a deep breath. "Right. Every day I'd come out of my flat with my friend, Rene. We shared a two-room flat over a shop in Newtown. We'd walk to the bus stop at the corner of our street then I'd continue on and catch the train at Newtown station. This man was often on the train. I'd certainly seen him before. He always smiled at me and said hello. I thought he was just being friendly. So, I was friendly back. We sat next to each other a couple of times, if there were seats, but mostly we stood."

"Did he tell you his name?" Lisa asked, hopefully.

"Yes, it was Peter."

"And a last name?" Gary interjected.

"No last name, just Peter."

"Go on," Lisa prompted.

"Anyway, one day he asked me if I wanted to go out with him that evening. He seemed pleasant enough and I said yes. He took me to a restaurant in Chinatown, then we walked up to see a movie near the Town Hall. He was really nice to me. He liked to touch, you know, put his arm around you, steer you through crowds, that type of thing. After the movie he suggested we walk home to my place. It was a bit of a long walk but I thought it would be nice: it was a warm night. There were lots of people out that night."

"Do you remember which restaurant you went to?" Lisa asked.

"Yes, it was the Golden Dragon in the Dixon Street Mall."

"Do you recall the movie or the theater?" Lisa followed up, wanting a more detailed account.

"Mmmmmm, it was an Australian film, *Man Tracks*! Yes that was it, *Man Tracks*." She smiled, pleased to be able to remember.

"That's good, Alice. Okay take it from where you started your walk home," Gary prompted her.

"We walked down George Street towards Broadway. He asked me if I would like a drink. I said okay, but only if he did. We went into a crowded pub, the Sportsmen's Hotel it was called. We ended up having quite a few drinks. Lots of people looked at us. You know, with me being black and him white. I got pretty drunk, so did he. When we left, I remember, I didn't want to walk home anymore but he insisted. He said it wasn't very far from the pub. But it was." Again she paused.

"Take your time, we've got all day," Gary said, softly.

"And all day tomorrow too, if you want," Lisa

said jokingly, in an attempt to ease the tension.

"Well, we came to the park near the university and he said it would be romantic to sit in the park and watch the lights of the city in the distance. So we did. We ended up near the university fence right out of the way. No one could see or hear us. I guess that's what we both wanted. Then he started." She shifted uneasily.

"It's okay. Take it real slow," Lisa said.

"We sat on the grass. He kissed me, hard kisses. I was surprised. He had been really quiet and gentle. He got angry with me, or something. I told him to stop, that I wanted to go home. He rolled on top of me, between my legs. He kept kissing me and moving on top of me. Then he pulled out a gun." She paused for a while, and Lisa held out her hand. They both waited patiently.

"He told me to take all my clothes off or he would kill me. He said it was a real gun and he began to swear at me. He got really angry and loud. He forced me to do things to him before he finally put his . . . penis inside me. When he finished he just stayed on top of me. He held the flat of the gun to the side of my head, on my ear. Then he made me suck the gun. He got hard again and this time he rolled me over and lifted me onto my knees and pushed it into my . . . arse. As he was coming this time he told me he was going to shoot me anyway." She stopped, swallowed, then continued. "Then he just did it. He put the gun against the back of my head and pulled the trigger. I woke up on the ground hours later. I couldn't believe I was alive. I was so relieved."

"Can you recall anything unusual about him? Does he limp, have any scars, tattoos; does he speak normally, anything?" Gary asked.

"No, nothing—he seemed pretty average."

"Did he say where he lived? Where he went to school?"

"No, but he told me he lived in the bush for a while when he was growing up. He didn't say where."

"What did you do after he shot you?" Lisa asked.

Now she started crying loudly. "I crawled to the nearest house and they called an ambulance . . ." she slumped in a pile, unable to continue.

Lisa moved and sat next to her; wrapping both arms around her she hugged her tightly. Gary switched the tape machine off.

Later, the doctor explained. "The bullet went in behind her ear and came out below her jaw on the opposite side. She is a very lucky, very brave young woman."

After the worst of the day's heat was over, Doctor Nick took Gary to the local swimming hole, along with Mitchell and five members of the football team. They all crowded into the back of the small Japanese utility truck.

Once they reached the men's swimming hole, Gary demanded confirmation that the freshwater pond was safe from crocodiles. They all laughed, stripped naked and dived in. Proof enough he thought, and followed suit. It was an idyllic tropical setting—palms swayed overhead and the creek widened out to a large billabong where brolgas strutted about. Lilies bloomed between large pads, which rippled across the previously still waters.

After they had swum and were relaxed, some of the Jirjorond men pulled huge slabs of clay from the banks of the pond and began to paint their bodies. One called Gary over to join them and he felt he could not refuse. With unashamed enthusiasm, the young man held Gary's arm and began to paint his naked body with white yellow and brown clays. Doctor Nick looked at Gary and smiled as he too became involved in the painting. Later, when the energy level was back to normal, they all dived back into the refreshing water. The traditional ephemeral artworks were soon washed from their bodies. Loud shouting and laughter drifted across the tropical landscape.

Doctor Nick suddenly looked seriously at Gary

and confessed that "Salty", the old salt-water croco-
dile, had paid a visit two days previously. He'd only
taken a playful dog that had carelessly ventured into
the incredibly light-green ocean. Gary looked
alarmed until Doctor Nick went on, a twinkle in his
eye, saying that one of the men had shot a monster-
sized male two months previously.

The afternoon ended with Doctor Nick showing
Gary some of the beautiful artworks from the hinterlands, for which the Queenslanders had become
world renowned.

When they arrived back in the village Lisa was
there, her hair still wet. She had been swimming also
but refrained from telling Gary anything about her
experience.

"Maybe I'll tell you sometime in the future but
not now. It's mine and I'm not sharing it with anyone," she said.

It was almost mandatory for everyone in the Weipa
community to attend the football team's send-off
at the canteen, and all five hundred Jirjorond
people and the entire European contingent of
eight were there. The country and western band
played loudly, but maximum gusto was reserved
for the rock & roll pieces in their repertoire.

Nick introduced the Sydney detectives to the

local schoolteacher, Marie, who told them to let her know when they wanted to head home. She was petite, blonde, thirty, single and very friendly. In the middle of her second year of a three-year term, she said she planned to see her contract out. She loved it here. They laughed and had a running joke about swimming with crocodiles through the entire evening.

Curious eyes followed Gary and Lisa everywhere, and there were cheers from the happy crowd when they pushed their way onto the dance floor. They danced self-consciously as the humid evening unwound.

Much later, in the cool of the evening, a number of people followed the doctor to his house for the much talked about barramundi barbecue. It was attended by some of the elders plus a handful of football players with their girlfriends and wives.

"You must come across some weird and wonderful medical cases up here," Gary said innocently, standing beside Nick as he worked on the large fish on the griddle.

"Yes I have. Medical neglect is the major problem. Some of those I'd rather forget," he said.

"Like what?" Gary pressed.

The doctor hesitated before replying. "On the northeast coast of Queensland I was called to visit

the home of an Aboriginal man who had pneumo-
nia. He told me he'd been to the local hospital the
previous night. The staff had let him sit in casualty
for hours because they thought he was drunk. He
begged them for help all through the night. Finally
he gave up and somehow dragged himself home to
bed. Someone called me and I found him there the
next morning. I called an ambulance. When it
arrived I asked the driver to take the patient to the
hospital and to make sure he received urgent attention. The driver said he didn't have the authority
to do that." Nick stopped briefly to baste the
browning fish. "I told him he bloody well did,
because of his training and position in the community. I said if medical attention was not
obtained he should report back to me immediately.
Only then was he attended to. He was lucky not to
have died."

"That's bloody terrible," Gary said angrily.

"Yes I know. You see, sometimes Aboriginal
patients who are ill are often regarded as drunk.
Diabetic coma is a good example. Diabetes is com-
mon among Aboriginal people, and a proper diagnosis is necessary."

"How can you stand it?" Gary asked seriously.

"It's not getting any better. I remember as a
young doctor when I first took on Aboriginal

patients. It was in Collarenebri in the fifties and six-
ties, at a time when one of the local policemen was
given the job of 'lock-up keeper'. His pay depended
on the number of prisoners in his cells."

"Don't tell me!" Gary interrupted.

"You guessed it. They used to raid the local
Aboriginal settlements arresting anyone, drunk or
sober. They charged them all with alcohol related
crimes, aggressive behavior and so on. One night the
cells were particularly empty. The raids were conducted and one of those arrested was a man who didn't
drink. He was woken from a deep sleep and taken in.
Later, in the cells he complained of chest pains. He
cried out, tortured for hours but was ignored. The
next morning he was found dead."

"Jesus!"

"It gets worse. I was called to do the autopsy. My
finding was clear, a coronary occlusion had been
present for a very long period, and it showed up
visually in the heart muscle. There was no alcohol in
his stomach. He could not have been drunk. That's
what I wrote in my report. The Inspector of Police
drove more than a hundred and fifty kilometers
from Moree to ask me to reconsider. He wanted me
to alter my report to say I'd been mistaken, that the
Aboriginal man did, after all, have alcohol in his
stomach."

"What did you do?"

"I refused. That's when he told me he could make life pretty tough for me out there."

"What! What did you do?"

"I pushed him out the door. Later at the inquest I presented my statement, unaltered. But you know there were no questions and no action was brought against anyone."

They both fell quiet.

Two hours later, when the barbecued seafood had been washed down by liters of fine white wine, the toll of a long, eventful day finally took hold of both Lisa and Gary. When Nick could see they were no longer able to hold up their end of the conversation, he suggested they might like to retire. They retreated quietly via a well-worn path from Nick's back garden to Marie's house.

Early next morning Lisa and Gary joined the twenty members of the football team on their DC-3 Cape Air charter flight to Cairns, where they would connect with a non-stop flight to Sydney.

It interested them both that although there were two Queensland state policemen serving the Weipa community, they saw them only twice, from a distance. They had never reported Alice's ordeal although it was widely discussed by everyone.

Gary was thirteen when his father passed away. It was very sudden, a heart attack. A cottage carpenter, he was working with one other man high on a frame installing roofing trusses when it happened. He fell forward onto the timber flooring five meters below. The scene looked messy, blood was everywhere, but he had died before he fell, according to the doctor.

At the funeral Gary was tight-mouthed. He forced himself not to cry. But tears spilled out of his eyes in spite of his wishes. He thought of the memories his father had left him.

When Gary was very young his father enrolled him at the Newtown Police Boys Club. Boxing was his dad's passion. His father's face was the mask of a well-seasoned fighter; after a career of twenty-eight fights for twenty-four wins, one draw and three losses, he was an above-average middleweight. He almost had a professional State title but he liked fighting mostly in tent shows. He travelled all over New South Wales and had at least two hundred tent fights. In the carnival sideshow atmosphere he would be pitted against heavyweights hooked in from the crowds. Abo bashing was a popular sport in the outback, racists would pay good money to see an Abo get a hiding. Who cared if they weren't evenly weighted? His father had decided that Gary would be a fighter too.

On the night of his first bout, when Gary was only six years old, his father was so nervous he left the gas fire on. The whole family had to go to watch Gary—his father insisted—which left the house empty. Inside the large gymnasium people hurried to get the best seats. It seemed ages until his bout was called but Gary was swept up in the competitive atmosphere. He was both excited and a little scared. When his event was called by the ring announcer, all motion seemed to slow. He could see everything with such clarity; his eyes were open wide.

His dad was in his corner. The bell rang and he pushed him forward. "Remember what I said mate . . . now do it!" he yelled after him. The crowd went crazy. Gary looked around the room. Smoke haze slowly rose from the packed seating area. Heads bobbed and turned. The boy opposite him had a nasty look on his face as they approached each other. The canvas underfoot was slippery. The referee cautioned them about not punching low and then the bell rang again.

Gary danced out from his corner, as he had learned, using the ring. His opponent chased him throwing wild punches, Haymakers, wide swings with both arms. Gary stopped and danced back the other way. He could hear his dad calling. At the very side of his vision he saw his father leaning under the bottom rope, pounding the floor with closed fists. "Don't run, fight him!" he yelled. "Fight him!"

A wild punch connected, Gary fell to the floor. As he shook his head, blood sprayed from his nose across his cheek. He looked at his father, he was laughing. He could not believe it. He was laughing! He leapt to his feet as the referee counted to three and danced after his opponent, looking for revenge. He began throwing straight lefts, jerking the boy's head back sharply as each punch connected. Tears came to his opponent's eyes; he didn't care. Gary's father had laughed at him! The lefts continued, the boy's head jerked, his shoulder-length blond hair exaggerated the motion. It wasn't long before the referee stepped between them and stopped the fight. Gary looked at his father who was almost delirious. His mother looked concerned, his brothers and sister cheered. He had won!

Although it had been a cloudless morning on the day of his father's funeral, the winter sun disappeared behind mounds of grey and it grew cold at the gravesite. People wept openly, both women and men. The rain started with a light sprinkling, but after ten minutes it fell in earnest. The service continued; the minister would not be deterred by the weather.

His father had been at Gary's last fight only ten days before. He didn't laugh anymore; he hadn't since Gary's ninth birthday. He had realized how serious the sport was to his son.

In recent years only his father went to his fights; the previous week his dad took him in the new family car. Gary felt pumped up, if he won this he would be eligible to fight in the elimination bouts for a State title next year.

His dad was in his corner. At the sound of the bell he pushed him forward. "Remember what I said mate. Now do it!" It was what he always said.

It was a tough fight. For the first two rounds Gary danced and jabbed. His opponent, an Italian boy from Leichhardt, kept coming at him. He had fast hands. Gary decided to match him for speed in the center—they exchanged short, fast blows. Gary managed to maneuver an uppercut between the blur of arms and fists, and he connected. The Italian boy fell heavily on his back, dazed, and was unable to continue. Gary looked to his own corner, his father was nodding, proudly clapping, his eyes welled with tears.

As his father's coffin was lowered slowly into the

grave, Gary knew the fight he had won the previous week was his last; he had only fought to please his dad. The rain came down more heavily as the service ended. The wind blew sweeping sheets of water across the small cemetery. Long after people left in their cars, Gary stood, thinking, deliberately drawing up memories of his father. He realized he needed enough to last him a lifetime.

Evelyn wasted no time in boarding a return flight to Sydney. She didn't mind admitting she was scared. The local police assured Christine they would keep a look out for the man, circulating a description immediately. Evelyn now feared he was stalking her.

From the air, the chain of beaches linked one to the other and carried on to the hazy horizon. The coastline unfurled beneath her, creating wonderful abstract patterns on which to reflect.

The taxi from Sydney Airport took only ten minutes to reach her house. Quickly taking her bags from the taxi trunk, Evelyn made her way inside, looking up and down the street before she banged the door shut.

She switched on every light in the house. "He knows where I live," she said out loud to no one. "He must, he stopped me twenty meters from here. He knows my name and he knows where I live."

She picked up the phone and dialled the local police. "Hello, I need some help . . . I believe I'm being followed by a man."

Five minutes later two police cars screeched to a halt in front of her house. The red and blue lights were left rotating, flashing out a warning to any hidden, would-be stalker as they spoke to Evelyn at her door. People peered from their homes wondering what crime required police action. Some came out and openly discussed it as they stood in dressing gowns and slippers. A third police car turned the corner and pulled in behind the others. Now they knocked loudly on Evelyn's door. It was some time before the door was opened.

"Thank you for coming so soon. Please come in," Evelyn gasped.

24

The red drapes hanging in Lisa's front window had broken loose and were at an angle. It was three in the morning; she had worked a late shift. As she let herself in the smell of cigarettes and beer hit her. Pizza cartons and stubby bottles of Sydney Bitter were strewn about the living room floor and mounds of cigarette butts spilled over the numerous ashtrays.

"My God!" said Lisa, screwing her face up. She could not contain her displeasure.

The kitchen was even worse. A card game, she thought. Cards had been thrown about fulfilling some drunk's anal scattering expression. It better not have been Alby she thought, furious. The lights in the kitchen would not switch on; a fuse must have blown. She sat down heavily in the dark room, tired, sad, lonely.

A siren sounded in the distance as Lisa bedded herself down on the couch for the night. She could not bear Alby after he had hosted one of these nights. "Yeah, that'd be right," she muttered as she picked up a pornographic videotape cover from the floor and placed it on the coffee table. She fell back onto the soft sofa and pulled a blanket over herself.

Lisa moved her hips, her arms and breasts floated as if they were on water. Suddenly she was sucked upwards into a white void. Once again, she stood naked in the familiar white tubular corridor.

"Lisa." The same soft voice called her. It was the naked black woman. "Be careful."

"Tell me who you are?" Lisa asked.

"Please be careful."

"Are you my mother?"

The water level rose rapidly.

"I can't stay."

Again the woman walked in the direction from which the water flowed then she faded into the white glow. Lisa was scared. The water was now at knee height.

"Come back!" she called after her. "Who are you? Are you my mother?" Again the walls beside her began to sag under the weight of the water. It pulled the roof section open. Overhead the blue sky beckoned. She climbed the webbing and the same few people peered in from above and reached for her, offering safety. The red-haired man finally reached her and with great strength he pulled her out of the way of the harmful water.

A loud knock at the door woke Lisa and Alby. Lisa was expecting no one and cared less about who it might be. Alby finally answered it taking delivery of a small package. Then he quietly retreated to the bedroom.

When he'd come back from Queensland Gary felt inspired, he created what he called a "scanning wall". He made it by fixing five meters of cork sheeting to the wall of the detectives' muster room. Then he started pinning material to the left top corner—photographs of victims and locations, maps, Identikit drawings, a detailed Modus Operandi. Lisa smiled when she saw what Gary was doing. Everyone from the section came to look. The material flowed in chronological order. By the end of the day he had finished, the entire board was covered. He sat back to admire his work along with about fifteen fellow detectives. He had created an object for a meditative-style fusion of mind, a focal point. Against another wall he installed a huge electronic white board that could supply photocopies if you pushed the appropriate buttons. Gary's idea was to encourage brainstorming; all leads were jotted on to the white board, a print taken, put on the main wall then acted upon.

The telephones in the large detective workspace were occupied more now than at any time since the Bondi killing. Gary's wall was having a positive impact. Everyone independently placed new pieces of information on the board overlaying the originals, superseding them.

Several days went by. The board had now taken on an organic life of its own, the collective consciousness style of problem solving which Aboriginal society had successfully applied for thousands of years had finally reached the high technological urban homicide squad of Sydney—"criminal dreaming"? For hours people sat dreaming, looking at the wall. Without speaking they would walk to the white board, write notes, take a photocopy, and leave the room. Later they would return to pin new material to the wall. Then they would sit, scan and dream, hoping the mysterious white light would flash in their brains again.

Lisa took her coffee into the room and sat so she could look at the center of the wall. Her peripheral vision saw the outer edges of material; her brain went onto Beta wave frequency. All sounds were blocked out. A white spot in the center of her mind's eye grew larger. She focused on it, transporting questions through it aimed at the mosaic of sheets pinned to the board. A small bright flash reflected back at her. Follow the light, her mother had told her long ago. Exactly when that was, she could not say but it was when she was very young. Slowly she focused on the room again, in her real time and place. She walked over to the board from where the light had flowed, fingering the two pieces of paper which contained reports of yet another man stalking an Aboriginal woman, the other was about the contrived meetings the Peter-suspect had with Alice from Weipa. She took them from the wall, smiling. "The light!" she said aloud as she hurried to share her find with Gary.

"What do you think?" she asked him.

"I think it's him," Gary said, finding it difficult to conceal his excitement. "Shall we talk to the lady?"

"But of course."

"Where does she live?" he asked as he read the sheet for the answer. He found it. "Redfern, about six or eight blocks from here."

Lisa asked, "Is she on the phone?"

"Yes," he said dialling. There was a pause. "Evelyn Bates? Detective Leslie here, I'd like to come and have a chat with you about the fellow you've seen following you. When would be a good time? Yes . . . yes, I have it here. Five o'clock would be perfect. Thank you." He hung the receiver on the cradle. "There . . . in half an hour. Is that soon enough for you?" He smiled warmly.

Lisa smiled back. She liked Gary; she liked working with him, being near him. She noticed women watching him, young and older females alike. Most Aboriginal men she knew were not as balanced as

Gary. He was sure about himself. He had manufactured a space in modern society for himself. He sat erect, straight-backed, his wide shoulders back.

"Cat got it?" he asked.

"What?"

"Your bloody tongue."

"No . . . five o'clock, great," she said. My God, he knows, she thought, I'm so transparent. She felt excited.

Precisely at five o'clock Gary shuffled his feet expectantly as Lisa knocked on Evelyn's front door. Evelyn called to them through the door.

"Who is it? Who's there?" she asked.

"Detectives Fuller and Leslie, I spoke with you on the phone earlier. You said to come at five. Would you like me to pass my badge under the door?" Gary spoke directly into the corner of the doorway.

"No, it's okay. Just a minute."

Several metallic clicks and slides sounded loudly through the door as Evelyn finally unlocked and disarmed her home security system. Once they were all seated, she told Gary and Lisa everything: the encounter on the street, the markets at Eumundi, the strange smile at the Eumundi hotel, being followed to Christine's house and how he had called to her by name. She didn't know the make of car he drove. She did agree the Identikit picture they showed her, while not a perfect likeness, could be the same man.

In the next room Gary called the office, he wanted a man left to watch Evelyn's house. Just in case he had followed her back to Sydney. The Queensland police didn't seem too interested in chasing up leads in Noosa. They were short staffed too.

"What do mean you can't spare one man! Jesus . . . you're amazing. Do you know that? I bet if she were white you'd find one wouldn't you? Yes, okay . . . I said yes!" He slammed the phone down.

"What was that all about?" Lisa asked, already knowing the answer.

"He said he didn't have enough men to investigate black deaths let alone live ones, the bastard."

The detectives asked their final questions and politely excused themselves. Evelyn showed them out, then, following her new routine, she secured herself indoors for the evening. Gary and Lisa looked up and down the street then walked briskly to the car and sped away, secure in the knowledge they were closer than ever to the rapist-murderer.

A raggedy vagrant sat, hunched forward, rolled in a ball in the doorway of a disused factory twenty meters away on the opposite side of the street. He smiled as the police drove away. "Ahhh, glad to see you Abos are back on the job," he murmured softly.

Lisa dropped Gary at his car. He went immediately back to stake out Evelyn's house himself; he knew in his water the man would come for her. It was just a matter of time.

Lisa reversed her car at the curb in front of her apartment, and glanced at the car clock as she straightened up. It was eight-thirty; she was physically and mentally spent after a long day, which had begun more then thirteen hours before. Cold winter rain fell in heavy vertical sheets driven angrily by a strong, gusty wind. She could barely see through her rear window and the side mirrors were of little use. She edged backwards again. Soon she was satisfied she was parked—there was no bump. Looking at how far she had to run to reach her front door she took a deep breath, flung the car door open and dashed into the torrential downpour.

Once inside her apartment she groaned. It was as she had left it that morning: scattered food cartons, cigarette-filled ashtrays, beer bottles—some left unfinished—the smelly remnants of the adult boys' bash. She rescued a pair of black panties from beneath the couch, frowning. She wasn't sure if they were hers. And if they were, what were they doing there? She went to the bedroom, tossed them into the laundry hamper, changed out of her clothes and went to the bathroom. Hot water from the shower rosette sprayed onto her face. She adjusted the temperature, adding more cold to the mixture then she lathered up and washed the city grime from her skin.

Toweling off in the bedroom, she sat on the bed. Next to her she noticed a package. She reached for it, turned it to read the label. It was addressed to Albert Bates. The front door opened; it was Alby.

"Is that you, Alby?" she called from the bedroom.

"Yeah, it's me."

"You're a bit late aren't you?"

"Yeah, I'm a bit late."

She could tell by his slurred speech that he had been drinking, again. "Have you been for a drink?"

He put his head around the doorway. "Yes, I've been drinking."

Lisa said nothing. She wanted to dress, she felt vulnerable. Quickly she stood up; it was too late, in two seconds he was next to her. He pulled the towel from her and stared at her naked body. His hands began to explore. She gently pushed at his chest.

"No, Alby . . . I'm too tired. I've had a long day." She was angry but tried to conceal it.

"Jesus, you're always tired," he said as he moved away, hurt.

"I found a pair of women's knickers in the living room—they're not mine!"

He left the room. "Well, they're not mine," he

said sarcastically. "Maybe they were from the last time we did it . . . a couple of weeks ago."

"A couple of weeks ago! That's not true." She chased after him. "Listen, we're not newlyweds. We don't have to prove ourselves sexually every night, do we?"

"Yes . . . we do!" he shouted.

Lisa was still a teenager when she first met Alby. After she fulfilled her contract on the Dean property at Cobar she stayed on for one more year. But the call of the city was too strong, the Cobar property too isolated. So, one month before her eighteenth birthday, she left the only family home she had known; her early childhood home was a distant memory.

Lisa was given addresses of people known to the Deans who lived in Sydney. She made a particular effort to find them when she arrived, clumsily navigating the confusion that was urban Sydney. The contacts were of little use; they feared she might want something from them. Oh, they were polite enough but offered nothing, certainly not what she had really come for: friendship.

After weeks of persistence, answering any job advertisement she thought she could fill, Lisa secured a chance interview for the New South Wales Public Service. Ostensibly she was thought suitable for a position as a clerk in the Department of Works then she sat an examination and an IQ test. When the results were released she was called to attend further interviews with various department heads of the Public Service. She had scored an average of ninety-seven percent over three subjects—third highest ever in the state—her IQ was put at 147. The Justice Department convinced her to join them. They said she could do some good for her people in their department; Lisa agreed. Her move to the police service, later, was not via normal channels.

A year later she met Alby beneath a large Moreton Bay fig tree in Sydney's Hyde Park. It was lunchtime; she was eating a sandwich while she read. He broke into her thoughts with his happy singsong voice. Standing with the cityscape as a backdrop he introduced himself. He worked for a large engineering firm. For weeks they met for lunch. He was city-born, a streetwise Koori. He took her to places in the city. She liked his strong, sure personality. Finally, he asked her to go with him for dinner and a show, at night. An official date, she thought, how romantic. She was swept up in the moment. Someone wanted her. She wanted desperately to belong, to join with convention.

Within a year they were married. She was twenty years old, he was twenty-two.

"What's in the package in the bedroom?" she asked, following him into the kitchen.

"Some tapes I sent away for, if you must know," he said, avoiding her gaze.

"What kind of tapes?" She knew. She felt she had lost him. She felt nauseous, inadequate.

He turned and walked up to her, lowered his face to hers and shouted. "Adult tapes!" Then he confessed. "Yes, there was a woman here last night. I broke the drought. So what!"

Within minutes Lisa was in the elevator carrying a heavy suitcase filled with hastily gathered clothing. In the car she fought back tears as she fumbled to find the ignition lock. It was impossible. Crying loudly, she slumped forward onto the steering wheel. Then, thumping the dash panel with a closed fist she screamed. "You fucking dickhead!" This was how Lisa showed her acceptance that their marriage had ended.

I came back to Sydney the next day after I saw Evelyn in Queensland. I knew I had to have her. It was risky but so is life. You could get hit by a bus at any moment, they reckon. The winter's almost over now anyway which is really why I left in the first place.

I told Colleen that Evelyn was a girl I used to go out with in Sydney. She was okay about it . . . she said she understood. I might go back when it gets cold, next winter. She was a bit pissed off about chasing them back to their house and me yelling out the car door and all that shit. But hey . . . ? We left on good terms. I gave her all the new furniture I bought when I first got up there— my TV and all the bedroom stuff. My three phony dole checks all came through at the same time so I had loads of money to buy that stuff with then. I miss her. She liked to mother me and I let her. It was good.

My mother never cared much about me. I still write to her. She's still in jail—seventeen years they gave her for killing the old man. The old bastard deserved it. He used to make her join in his sex orgies. Christ, you couldn't blame her for not want- ing to fuck him and his poofta bisexual mates. She wouldn't tell me about it but I knew. Even when I was little I knew that sometimes there were more than two people in their bed at night. I heard he had his poof mate up his arse when she shot them.

I'm glad she did him in. Even though she's paying for it now, I think she feels it was worth it. Some smart bastard once said, be prepared to do the time if you do the crime. I think that's a pile of bullshit but mum doesn't. She's due for release when she's sixty-two.

25

It was a crisp autumn morning. Brilliant sunshine filled the trees, highlighting the colorful leaves, the shadows equally dark on the undersides. The car started the instant the key was turned. Alan Jackson had decided to return to the office. He had been delaying it for some time. His doctors had, too. He had been on a low salt, fat-free diet for weeks. At first rest was essential then, slowly, he had increased his exercise. He would walk a mile down to the river and back every morning. In the afternoon he walked a mile in the other direction, away from the river, and back for dinner at six o'clock. He faithfully took his Digitalis, which was supposed to strengthen his heart muscle as well as the diuretic, Frusemide. He was very diligent in maintaining his potassium levels too. The car felt good under his touch. The familiar route to work was a comfort to him.

Alan smiled as he thought about getting back to work and seeing his old friends again. But suddenly a sharp pain stabbed at his left arm, shoulder and chest. It took all the breath from his lungs. The severe cramp-like pain forced his legs and arms to twist. The car sped across the center line and ploughed head-on into a delivery van. He heard the sound of metal giving way, glass shattering, pieces of car attachments hitting the roadway as the violent impact set his seatbelt into lock mode. He slipped on his seat, the door folded against his hip, deeply gashing him as it forced him sideways. The steering wheel pushed against his chest. He felt his sternum give way as the plastic wheel snapped, the metal column pushed under his chest plate piercing his right lung.

The ambulance arrived seven minutes from the time of notification. Alan was still alive. The efficient uniformed men soon had him on a stretcher inside the St. Johns ambulance van. Weaving through the rush hour traffic they sped towards the hospital, the screaming siren signalling their approach. Heroic methods had to be employed during transit as Alan became comatose. He arrived at the emergency admittance entrance hooked to machines; there he was skillfully transferred onto bigger machines. His family was notified immediately. The medical staff around him knew the machines would be switched off and all treatment would cease before nightfall. They had decided, at five-thirty, precisely ten hours from now, Alan Jackson would be allowed to die.

Gary was eventually successful in securing a stakeout, just one man, for Evelyn's house. He had arranged things so that Evelyn called Redfern police station to tell them when she was at home. Within minutes a car would roll to a stop out front. And Gary was again able to be home at night with his family.

Helen answered the knock at the door dressed in a baggy tracksuit. Soft piano music emanated from the living area behind her. There was a reddish glow from an electric fire in a corner; the walls were bathed in warm, low-level lighting, which spilled from three matching lamps.

From where Gary sat he could not see who Helen was speaking to. He stood up, still holding a magazine in his hand. "Who is it?" he asked. Then he saw the tearful figure of Lisa in Helen's arms, her suitcase sat on the veranda outside the open door. "Oh Jesus, come in quickly, close the door," he said. He carefully squeezed by them, took the suitcase up and closed the door himself. Helen released her grip on Lisa as she fell into Gary's arms. He pulled her to him firmly, reassuringly. She buried her face into his shoulder, hiding her tears.

"Sit down," Helen said after some time. "Do you want to talk about it?"

She shook her head. "No."

"It's okay, it's okay, don't worry," Gary said.

Without saying another word Helen moved to the kitchen to prepare a pot of tea. Gary led Lisa to the couch. David strayed into the kitchen after his mother, rubbing his eyes, half asleep.

As they sat she again fell in his arms, her head hung low, tears streamed down her cheeks. Lisa formed her mouth to speak—wetness clung to her lips. "Shit, I feel so bloody stupid," she said. She darted her tongue onto her outer lips and rolled them together.

"You're not stupid," Gary reassured her.

"The bastard." She stopped, unable to say more. She was embarrassed.

Helen carried David back to bed.

"Look, it's really okay. You don't have to say anything. We understand. You can stay here," Gary said, managing a crooked smiled. She looked at him.

"Fuck him anyway," he whispered. They both laughed nervously, eroding some of the tension from the moment.

Helen came back to the room with a fully laden tea tray. "That sounds better," she said. As she began pouring the chamomile tea, its bittersweet scent rose with the steam and quickly filled the room.

"I'm not going back to him. It was a mistake from the beginning. We got caught up emotionally. We were both too young."

"Stay here until you get on your feet. We can car pool—save on petrol. You know, ride to the office together."

"Sure! That will give the scandalmongers at work some real fuel. It would be enough to last them for weeks. You can just imagine what they'd be saying."

"Who cares what they say?" Helen chimed in.

Lisa looked at Gary. "What have you been telling Helen about our workmates?" she asked. She let out a huge sigh. Her body went limp, she felt herself relaxing. She sipped at the hot tea wondering about her future, then Gary gently squeezed her knee. She looked up at him and forced a smile.

Alan Jackson's funeral service was long and tedious. So many people wanted to eulogize him that they had to be carefully stage-managed. The Church of England minister asked speakers to adhere to a five-minute time limit and he restricted the number of speakers to six. His own part in the service however, had no such limit.

At the gravesite Lisa moved to Gary's side. "I've got an apartment. I'll be moving out tomorrow," she whispered. They turned towards each other and smiled.

After the funeral, a crowd gathered at the Redfern Tavern—Jackson's longest-serving officers agreed he would have wanted them to hold his wake there. Each had a story about the "old man". If you passed around the large barroom you could hear his life's work encapsulated. Along with some of the more amusing or embarrassing moments, numerous acts of heroism were recalled.

"I didn't get to know him very well but he sorted me out very quickly," Gary said to a large group seated and standing around a booth. Their table was covered with glasses; thirty-five at least, mostly empty. It would be a long session. Lisa sat across from Gary listening intently to accounts of Jackson's earlier times in the force. Gary told those near him about the private discussions he had with the "old man". Gary felt very aware of Lisa. Now that she had her own apartment he would miss her, he liked her living with him. He liked their new informality. He liked seeing her dressed in pajamas, or running from the bathroom with a towel loosely draped about her, her hair dripping wet. They now had a more personal, more intimate relationship, and that was what he would miss. As he watched her now, her perfectly painted lips parted, her white evenly shaped teeth showing through, he became excited.

"Lisa," he called to her. She looked up. He gestured to her to meet him at the bar. "Let's get the drinks in," he said loudly above the din.

They walked across to the crowded bar.

"I'm really going to miss you," he said as he leaned onto the bar.

"Come on! You'll still see me every day. How could you possibly miss me?" But she knew exactly what he meant. They both fell quiet. He ordered the drinks; she slid an arm around his waist and moved her hip against him. They didn't speak. The drinks arrived; they organized a tray to put them on and made their way back to the table.

Later, after agreeing they were too intoxicated to drive, Lisa and Gary telephoned for a taxi to take them home. It was already three in the morning; the number of people at the wake would in no way be noticeably reduced by their absence.

Gary opened the door of the cab and slid in beside Lisa. She took his hand and held it for the entire journey home. They spoke jokingly about the evening, her new apartment, which was three blocks from the office, and Helen. Each played down their heightened emotions. Lisa wondered if their precious friendship would be jeopardized by the living arrangements they had shared these past few days. As the taxi pulled up in front of the house she leaned across and kissed Gary on the cheek and squeezed his hand.

Inside the house they both skillfully avoided being too close to the other. Lisa went to the guest room. Gary looked in on his sleeping wife and child then sat on the couch and flicked the television set on. Lisa scurried to the bathroom in her pajamas. When she came out she softly whispered her good-night across the room to Gary. He didn't react.

"Good night," she said once again, more loudly.

"Good night," Gary replied. He smiled politely then sat back to watch an American news program, which was beamed live to Australia via satellite.

Lisa lay on her side under a down-filled quilt. She felt a warmth flow over her. Again she was sucked upwards into the white void. She stood naked as a soft voice called to her.

"Lisa." It was the naked black woman. "*Please* be careful," she said.

The water level rose rapidly.

"Who are you?" Lisa asked frustrated.

The woman walked in the direction from which the water flowed. Lisa was scared. The water was now at knee height. She looked up. The red haired man offered his strong arm to her. It was Mr. Chapman!

She recalled his face now, from the Bombala hostel.

"Come back mother!" she called after the woman. Again the walls beside her began to sag under the weight of the water. It pulled the roof section open. Overhead the blue sky beckoned. Mr. Chapman reached even lower into the white tube for her. She turned away from him and ran after the woman, her mother, who was in the distance but still visible. Then she woke with a start. Sitting upright in bed, she broke into a cold sweat. Too much drink, she thought. She lay down again, forcing the dream back to her mind, for once she wanted to complete it satisfactorily. The visions took on a plastic hardness. Not real dreaming at all, she thought. Then she faded once more to sleep.

Four hours later Helen woke Gary from a deep sleep on the couch. The television blared out a commercial as she steered him to bed.

When Colleen saw Peter's Identikit face on television she called the Noosa police immediately. The report was faxed to Sydney within thirty seconds of her signing it. Ten seconds later Lisa read it and spoke with her by phone.

"Are you certain it's the same man you know?" Lisa asked.

"Yes, I'm certain. I should know: I lived with him for months."

"Where was that?'

"At my current address here in Queensland."

"What's his name?"

"Peter . . . Peter Simpson."

Lisa felt an adrenaline rush at the name. It was the same. "Did you ever see his driver's license?"

"No."

"Did he have a passport?"

"I don't think he had one. If he did, I never saw it. But I know he did use other names. He used the names of racetracks. He said he did it to dodge the taxman."

"Colleen please don't take any offense at this, but did he have sex with you in an unusual way or use any unusual things?"

There was a long pause. "He had a handgun." She was embarrassed but continued. "He used to rub it in me. You know, just playing. He made me suck it too but it was always empty of bullets. I can't believe it." She paused again. "He's that killer isn't he?"

"We can't be sure but it sounds like you're lucky to be able to call him your ex-boyfriend," Lisa said emphatically. "If he should call you *please* try to find out where he's living. If it is him, it's important to stop him now. He's been out there for a long time, doing it for years."

A chill spread throughout Colleen's body; she shifted in her seat. There was a long silence.

"Hello, Colleen . . . are you there?" Lisa held the phone close and spoke down into the receiver.

"I'm here."

"We will stay in touch with you and please call me if he contacts you. You can reach me any time, day or night, at this number."

"Yes, okay, I will."

Lisa replaced the telephone. She felt physically elated; the cordon around Peter Simpson was closing. The phone rang.

"Hello, Lisa Fuller speaking."

"Hello, Lisa. This is your mother."

26

The phone made a loud crash as Lisa let it drop to the floor. She began to shake; her hands were not capable of holding anything. She reached for the telephone again and brought it to her ear.

"Hello, are you there, Lisa?"

"Yes . . . I'm . . ." She could not speak, her throat had closed, muscles moved involuntarily, sealing off all possibility of speech; she had lost the ability to carry on. She looked incredulously at the circular holes in the phone piece as if her mother would materialize from them at any moment.

Making a supreme effort, she swallowed a massive lump in her throat and continued to speak. "Hello . . . mother?" There was a pause. "Please, are you really my mother?"

"Yes baby, I'm your mother."

Both women began to weep.

The *Australia Today* television program had sent an advance crew to reconnoiter an upcoming special two weeks prior to the live telecast. The producers intended to stage the show in the center of Sydney. It was spring, so they planned to go outdoors and feature the Botanical Gardens, the Opera House, the massive Harbor Bridge as well as the waterways of the deepwater harbor. Two days previous to the show's telecast the big outside broadcasting vans rolled to a stop beside the steps of the Opera House. Staging trucks carrying set pieces, furniture and plants followed the lighting vans. All were unloaded, set up, secured. Thick cables ran in a line from control van to set. With one day to airtime, broadcasting test signals were relayed to the studios. Stand-in announcers and extras sat at desks and mumbled into microphones, enabling technicians to finely tune voluminous pieces of equipment. The two-hour program began live at seven every morning; and so it did the following morning.

The first half hour of the program was flawless.

"Welcome back, it's twenty past the hour." Ross Fleischman turned his head to look into another camera, reading from an autocue machine. "Over the past several years the incidence of murder-rape crimes in New South Wales has risen sharply. The police feel this is due largely to one man. An organized hunt for one particular suspect has been in operation for the past eight months. Investigating units have combined with a newly formed Aboriginal task force in an effort to track down the serial killer responsible. With me is Detective Gary Leslie who is from that Aboriginal task force. Good morning, Detective Leslie. May I call you Gary?" Fleischman asked.

"Good morning, Mr. Fleischman. Yes, you can call me Gary if I can call you Ross."

"It's a deal, my friend. Let me ask you, how close are you to catching this maniac?"

"Very close. Obviously we can't divulge any information on television but I can tell you we have compiled a fact sheet on these murders that is the most comprehensive ever in this country. New techniques are being employed; aided by modern technology we are creating methods which give us the ability to cross-reference information with most police stations in the country, instantly." Gary looked to Lisa standing behind the cameras. She nodded her approval.

"You've got some photos to show our viewers," Fleischman said before looking over to the control room to the director. "Can we see those please, Hugh?" He looked at the TV screen that was placed beside the cameras for quick reference. "There . . . on the screen now. That is the face of a murder-rapist. If you know this man or have seen him recently, contact your nearest police station immediately. Is that right, Gary?"

"Yes Ross, but remember this man is dangerous. He has killed many times before. He will think nothing of doing it again, so please don't try to apprehend him yourself. Call your local police station, let us take control of it."

"Okay, we'll all keep a look out for him, Gary. Thank you for coming in today and talking with us." Fleischman turned to face another camera. "Coming up next, we've got a man who says his dog talks to his cockatoo. We'll be back right after this short break."

The floor manager called loudly across the location set. "Clear! We're into commercials."

Ross Fleischman leaned across and shook Gary's hand. "Good luck, hope we've been of some assistance."

"Thank you."

"You can leave now. We are on a commercial break."

"Uh, yeah right." Gary looked over his shoulder. A man with an English sheep dog and a white cockatoo smiled at him. Gary realized he was waiting for him to vacate the chair. He jumped up quickly, smiling, embarrassed.

Gary heaved a sigh of relief, relaxed his muscles

and walked over to join Lisa on the other side of the cameras. "I suppose it went okay," he said soliciting a response.

Lisa obliged. "You were great."

Gary turned and looked back to the stage set. "I really want to see this." He scoffed. "A dog and a parrot, talking."

The scene for the interview area was situated against a large glass section of the Opera House. Suddenly Gary saw a man reflected in the glass panels behind Ross Fleischman. He was standing on a hill, his hands placed defiantly on his hips.

"It's him!" Gary said out loud. Lisa knew immediately what he meant. They both turned to face him. He taunted them with an upturned finger while he stood safely on the other side of five hundred television spectators on a rise leading to the Botanical Gardens.

"I've got to try," Gary said and he was off. Lisa also took up the chase. Gary pushed and shoved people as he gathered pace. Simpson saw him and took off through the gates into the gardens proper.

Gary wound his way up five flights of stone stairs and leaped over the wrought-iron fence at the top onto a grassy slope. He caught a glimpse of the blue sweater Simpson was wearing as he darted between bushes a hundred meters away. "Arsehole," he spat through gritted teeth. Reaching a pace he could maintain, he fumbled with his coat, pulling his arms from the sleeves, he heaved it onto the garden lawns. He ran at an angle to reduce the distance between them. Ahead he picked a spot where he could scale another fence, which he thought would pull back even more ground between them. He ran hard at the spot, put a hand on the top and cleared the two-meter-high fence with ease: now Simpson was only fifty meters ahead. Simpson looked back; Gary smiled at him but he was hurting inside. His thighs pained as lactic acid drained into them, they were underused. He ignored it, pumping his arms he forced himself to chase harder, faster. The paved walkway was slippery under foot. Simpson almost fell as he slid negotiating a sharp turn in the path.

Gary cut the corner running through the precious garden growth, crushing exotic tropical species underfoot as he did so. Simpson was shocked to see Gary only thirty meters behind and gaining. Then, as Gary rejoined the path, he slipped, falling heavily and careering into a garbage bin, spilling its contents over himself as well as the perfectly kept lawns.

He jumped quickly to his feet but fell again: he had torn a hamstring at the back of his left thigh. Simpson disappeared behind the glass pyramid at the end of the garden's grounds.

After a while Lisa was at Gary's side. "You almost had the bastard!" she said. Lisa was fit but not a runner. There was no way she could run Simpson down. Taking several deep breaths, she put a hand under Gary's arm and helped him to his feet. "Are you okay?" she asked, frowning, looking at his ripped, soiled trousers.

"No!" he said angrily.

27

Evelyn called an extraordinary meeting at the
Aboriginal Dance Company. She arrived early with
Rosie and two of the office staff and they switched on
the lights and proceeded to arrange seating in the
huge upstairs rehearsal hall. At seven-thirty they
were joined by the full company of dancers. Slowly
she walked to the front to face the group. She shuffled her notes nervously and began.

"Danny Renaldo started this company with a
simple view that it would provide a place for
Aboriginal dancing to be practiced by Aboriginals.
His passing must not hinder that dream. A few people who assisted Danny decided to hold this meeting
to find a way to keep the company going. We are prepared to take on the responsibility if you want us to.
There are several people who want to speak so I'll
pass the floor over to them." Evelyn was concise.

The meeting was orderly, sometimes solemn.
The discussion finished with Evelyn being voted to a
two-year term as Artistic Director/Choreographer.

The next few months would be crucial for her. She had to create at least one new work for public viewing every six months. She was so excited. She locked the empty building as she had done for years and proceeded across the busy street into the park.

She was more than halfway through Prince Alfred Park before she realized how late it was. She turned, defensively looking about, then increased the rate of her gait. Ahead she could see two lovers on a bench. To her left two derelicts were swearing at each other beneath a tree. In the distance, in the shadows, a man was urinating against a fence. A fire siren could be heard far off.

As she continued walking, she heard someone approaching from behind. She turned quickly—it was the man. He walked briskly too, with purpose. He was not drunk. She broke into a slow jog. The man behind her walked faster. She turned, it was definitely him, and he was gaining on her!

"Leave me alone!" she screamed at him. Her body was pumping, flowing with adrenaline. She sprinted the two hundred meters to the end of the park; plus a further three hundred meters to her home, leaving the man far behind.

Evelyn breathed heavily as she secured herself in her house. She picked up the phone. Dialling the police she fell heavily into a chair. Lisa and Gary were seated in her living room five minutes later as a police car patrolled the area, finding nothing.

I'm getting a bit pissed off with these Abo cops! I thought if anyone would understand what it's like being the underdog, they would.

He nearly caught me in the Botanical Gardens the other day. I just went down to watch the Australia Today show. They said all last week if anyone wanted to come and see the show being done at the Opera House they could. So I went. But when I saw the Abo cops I thought I'd better watch from a distance. Then the Abo bloke actually went on the fucking show, it was a laugh really but not the part when he chased me. That black bastard can run. I thought that it was all over for me baby. No, I laughed when they were talking about me and there I was, right next to them. Like now, they're inside there and I'm only across the fucking street.

"Even though we have a man out front when you're home . . . for better security. As we mentioned to you before, you really should move in with friends," Lisa told Evelyn.

"Yes, I will . . . you're right."

"Today?" Gary was pushing.

"Yes, today. I promise."

"One of our men is stationed out front now. If you feel settled we'll leave," Lisa said. "My new apartment is around the corner from here so I'll leave my address and phone number. You can call me any time."

"That's very kind of you," Evelyn said.

"I don't think you'll be bothered with him again tonight but you know we can get here real fast if you call again," Gary offered.

Evelyn smiled. "Thank you both," she said.

The front door spilled light onto the darkened footpath as it opened. Lisa and Gary continued to chat with Evelyn at the door. They didn't notice the shadow moving in the doorway opposite.

"Remember, we are close by."

"Thanks again," Evelyn said as she closed he door.

Lisa waved to the policeman seated in the car in front of Evelyn's house as she and Gary got into their car. The shadowy figure opposite shifted slightly as the Aboriginal cops drove away.

The following morning Lisa switched her computer on and lit a cigarette. She highlighted the heading: Medical Search. After the heading: Name, she typed: Simpson, Peter. The computer whizzed and whirred, clicked and buzzed. Then an electronic ring sounded out: it matched!

"Gary look here," she called. He came up behind her and looked at her screen.

Lisa typed: More Information Required. The computer whirred again, then clicked to stop more quickly than before, it chimed a single electronic note. The screen flashed, words scrolled up the screen: Penrith Hospital, Patient, Surgery Left Ankle; Motorcycle accident victim, admitted unconscious, manipulate ankle, set in plaster. It stopped and whizzed, the fan clicked into cooling mode.

"What do you think?" she asked Gary.

"Ask it for more again."

Lisa typed: More Information Required. The computer whirred again and sounded its find: ding! The screen brightened again: Pathology testing carried out at Sydney Hospital Laboratories.

"We've got to know if the sample is still available," Gary said.

Lisa typed: More Information Required. The computer whirred, whizzed clunked then flashed: Simpson, Peter—Biopsy tissue currently with Sydney Hospital Laboratory, Macquarie Street, Sydney.

"Yes!" Lisa exclaimed loudly as she punched the air.

Lisa immediately ordered the tissue to be DNA tested. The DNA readout taken from the sperm found on four dead women was compared to that of the Peter Simpson specimen.

A few hours later that night, the results were faxed to her. They matched!

The Women's Detention Center at Parramatta was constructed on a ridge overlooking a beautiful river ravine one hundred and twenty-seven years ago. The historic city had several goals built there since early European occupation. The numerous willows, which wept beside the fast-flowing waters of the river, were clearly visible from Ruby Simpson's cell. As she lit a cigarette the early morning sun streamed past the small bars of her window cutting lines through the bluish smoke.

Ruby was a short shapely woman in her late forties. Her straight hair hung to her shoulders and curled outwards. The prison uniform did not detract from her full figure. Hard drinking had taken its toll on her skin, giving it a fragile jaundiced appearance. She was startled to hear her cell door being opened. She puffed hard on her cigarette.

"Come on Ruby, someone to see you," the female warder said.

"To see me? Who'd want to see me?" she asked.

"You'll see."

"Cops! I bet it's cops. They know all about me already. I've done nothing else. Geez, what the hell do they want now?"

They walked slowly along the corridor of stone, through two gates and a tall steel door— they all had to be locked and unlocked. This was a maximum security facility. Soon they arrived at an interview room usually reserved for lawyers and clients.

"Hello. Are you Mrs. Ruby Simpson?" Ross Fleischman asked.

"Yes, that's right," Ruby said. She could not place his familiar face.

"I'm Ross Fleischman, Mrs. Simpson. May I call you Ruby?"

"Yes, that's okay." Then she remembered. "You're on television aren't you?"

"That's right Ruby. That's what I've come to see you about—"

There was a knock at the door. The same warder had come back with a five-man camera crew. "You can set up over here fellas," Fleischman called to the technicians. "If that's okay with Ruby."

Ruby's felt nervous, embarrassed, she pushed at errant strands of hair which had fallen across her forehead. She nodded her approval.

A lone white cockatoo spread his wings wide as he slowed and landed high in a tree in Helen's back-yard. She watched from her kitchen window. It was the weekend. The solitary bird cawed loudly across the valley. Soon, the sky above her garden went white with the arrival of a whole flock of cockatoos, then they began to chatter. There was some nervousness in the gathering: in the lower branches ten or more birds rotated, changing position, changing stems. The flock became unbalanced, their anxiety transmitted to the others. One solitary bird flew away. After a brief time he called across the valley. Several answered his call and then suddenly they were off, the spreading of so many wings was dramatic as the entire flock took flight. The trees were empty once more.

Helen sighed, then continued preparing the coffee and returned to the bedroom.

"What was that racket out the back?" Gary asked her.

"It was beautiful, a whole flock of huge white cockatoos landed in our trees. There must have been thirty or more."

"Sounded like five hundred."

"It was wonderful." Helen had been moved. She sat on the bed and continued. "I went to see Dr. Peg yesterday."

"Why, what's wrong?" Gary sat upright in the bed, concerned.

"There's nothing *wrong*," she assured him quickly, then she smiled. "I'm pregnant, that's all. We're going to have another little bubba."

Gary leapt out of bed and, standing on the bed in

all his nakedness, he cheered to the sky. "Yahoo! You bloody beauty!" He bounced off the bed onto the floor, swept Helen up in his arms and danced an exaggerated polka around the small room.

Helen had been unsure how Gary would react to her news. Overnight she had created numerous scenarios of this moment in her mind. She much preferred this version.

Three hours later, Gary, Helen and little David were on the Harbor Bridge driving north. They had packed a picnic hamper with Palm Beach in mind as a good spot to spend a warm spring afternoon. The car radio played upbeat music and Gary tapped the steering wheel sitting at a red traffic light. He turned to Helen and said. "I just realized I made love to a pregnant woman last night."

"If you play your cards right you might get lucky again." Smiling, she looked straight ahead.

"Shhh," Gary chided her playfully. "Someone is listening in the back seat." But David sat in his car seat, looking at a dog in the car beside him, mesmerized.

The traffic was more dense as they drew closer to the golden sands of Sydney's northern surfing beaches. At Newport, Gary pulled the car to a stop and bought some chilled wine. The unseasonable sunshine had attracted like minds to the coast. A lack of sufficient parking space at Palm Beach meant leaving the car for a long walk to the ocean. Gary and Helen could not care less; they were swept up in prenatal euphoria.

Winter's chill was still present in the spring air as Lisa drove over the Blue Mountains west of Sydney. Her mother now lived in the small town of Mudgee. The weekend reunion was quickly arranged, both were anxious to see the other. Coming off the steep slopes into Lithgow she felt excited, nervous. Then she saw the large green sign indicating she should turn right— it spelled, in huge white letters: Mudgee. Riding the rim of the deep Capertee Valley, Lisa tried to remember her mother's face. What would she look like? Would she recognize her? The only memory she held of her mother was a contorted, pleading face peering through the window of the police car as it spirited her away all those years ago.

She pulled up in front of a small fibrolite-brick house with a red tile roof. A gum tree stood tall in the front yard, the lawn was well-kept. Simple flowers: poppies, snapdragons and pansies bloomed from beds, which surrounded the house. Before Lisa could leave her car, the front door opened. A shapely, middle-aged, dark-skinned woman peered around the doorframe. Then, as Lisa closed the car door, she slowly ventured onto the veranda. They met each other at the gate, falling into a long, tight embrace—neither was able to speak. With clear certainty both knew the other. Non-verbal bonding—created in early childhood—had surfaced. Both cried tears of happiness. The government's deeply inflicted wounds, the forced separation of mother from daughter, at last could begin to heal.

In the hours that followed, Lisa's mother told her about her father who had died in a car accident aged thirty-one, and about her only sibling, a brother. Photo albums were produced and people identified. Lisa was spellbound; more than once tears blocked her vision. Most of her cousins were married and lived in Sydney. Her mother had had her brother with a second husband who she had divorced ten years ago. Her brother was three years younger than Lisa. His name was Paul Ferguson, he was gay and worked in show business, changed his name to Danny Renaldo. She lost contact with him once he moved from Sydney to dance with the Australian Ballet in Melbourne.

Some movement was visible though the dark, early morning at the Network Eight Television Station. Its Sydney studios were slowly coming to life with the arrival of the technical, camera, lighting and make-up crews. The producers and on-camera presenters pulled up soon after. The once dark studio was now ablaze with a hundred and sixty foot-candles of light. The lighting director sat in every presenter's seat, in turn, with his light meter, calling the level via a talk-back facility to his dimmer switching crew in the control room. The levels were adjusted perfectly to his reading. Other staff members were shouting instructions across the large studio. Fresh flowers were required in all vases, had they arrived? Yes they had. Had anybody seen Ross Fleischman? He's in make-up, came the reply. The closer to seven o'clock the more frantic the shouting became. But all was in readiness despite the hyperactive veil of confusion.

The director, the five-star general, finally called his troops to arms. His voice boomed from overhead speakers. "Tense up, everybody! We are on the air in ten seconds."

Everyone did a mental countdown from ten. At five another announcement: "Five seconds. Panic stations!" the director called to his infantry.

A floor manager, standing beside a camera, held five fingers high for all to see. The signature theme music could be heard faintly. The fingers were reduced by one every second. When all fingers and thumb were gone he pointed to the camera. A red light flashed on top of it and Fleischman's face sprang to life.

28

Gary hurtled in from the bathroom when he heard Peter Simpson's name used in the introduction to the next segment on the *Australia Today* television show. Lying on the couch with the remote control unit, Helen increased the volume.

". . . yesterday morning I was in the Parramatta Women's Prison. It was there I met with and taped the following interview with Peter Simpson's mother. Simpson is accused of killing at least one white and three Aboriginal women. Have a look at this."

The videotape was sent rolling. Fleischman and Ruby Simpson were seated in the interview room of the prison.

"I have with me this morning Mrs. Ruby Simpson. Mrs. Simpson is the mother of serial killer-rapist Peter Simpson. Good morning

Mrs. Simpson."

"Good morning Mr. Fleischman," Ruby said shyly. She looked directly into the camera lens even though Fleischman was seated beside her.

"Mrs. Simpson . . . may I call you Ruby?"

"Yes, certainly."

"Ruby, police have evidence that your son may be a killer and a rapist. How does that make you feel?"

"I don't know really."

"Do you feel anger, pain, shock, remorse?"

"No . . . not really . . . I didn't do those things, he did."

"No, of course we know you didn't do them but your son allegedly did. How does it feel to know that you may have raised Australia's most prolific murderer?"

"I don't feel anything. I suppose I feel a bit nervous."

Fleischman shifted uneasily on his seat, the interview was not going well.

"If you had to raise your boy over again would you do anything different?"

"I don't know."

"Mrs. Simpson, Ruby, have you anything to say to your son if he is watching this morning?"

"Yes . . . I would like to say something to

him." She looked at the camera again. It slowly zoomed in to frame a tight close-up shot of the tired-looking prisoner. "Petey, you've got to stop. Go to the cops . . . give up. Don't do any more killing. Stop it now!"

Fleischman smiled. Thank God she came good, he thought.

Helen turned the sound on her television down.

"It might just work," Gary said hopefully. He walked to the bedroom to finish dressing. Helen continued to watch the show.

Suddenly Helen called, "Gary look. Quickly!"

In the television studio, Fleischman held a telephone to his ear. "Yes, Peter, we understand you are quite a bit different to the rest of us," Fleischman said patronizingly.

"He's actually talking to Simpson on the phone!" Helen said excitedly.

"Jesus!" Gary said as he reached for his own phone. He dialed emergency. "Detective Gary Leslie, Homicide Squad here, I need to be connected immediately to the Channel Eight television studios, this is an emergency."

"Channel Eight is Great. Good morning, I'm Stephanie how may I help you?" the telephonist asked.

"Detective Leslie here, Sydney Homicide Squad, I need to speak to Mr. Fleischman now!"

"I'm sorry sir that's impossible. We have strict instructions from our Head of News, not to disturb Mr. Fleischman while he is taking the Simpson call."

"Put me through on another phone, now! You will be charged with aiding a felon if you don't connect me!" Gary was livid. He wanted to ask Fleischman to keep talking while he traced the call.

"That call has been completed, I can connect you now Detective Leslie."

"Jesus . . . don't bother!" Gary slammed the phone down.

Later the same day in the office Lisa, Gary and a large group of detectives watched a replay of the Fleischman–Simpson telephone call.

"I would never have gotten this far if I wasn't a bit unique," Peter Simpson's voice said over a speaker as the television picture showed Fleischman contorting his facial muscles in an attempt to look intelligent.

"Rrr-ight, yes Peter," Fleischman said.

"So if and when I give myself up to police, it will all have to be on my terms. Do you understand?"

"Yes Peter, I understand perfectly. When do you think that will be and what are your terms?" Fleischman had his scoop. He could not hold this serious face for much longer, he wanted to leap and yell with joy.

"I haven't decided yet."

"Well, will you call me when you do, Pete?"

Everyone knew he should not have called him Pete; he had overstated his eagerness to befriend the killer. The director groaned in the control room; some of the infantry on the studio floor turned their backs from Fleischman to conceal their raised eyebrows and twisted smiles.

"I don't know . . ."

A loud buzzing followed as the telephone line went dead. Fleischman was quick to fill the gap. "Well there you have it: another *Australia Today* exclusive. For those of you who joined us late, Peter Simpson's mother appealed for her son to give himself up in an interview we pre-recorded yesterday. Simpson called me seconds ago and I spoke with him in person, live. We need to take a quick break. Back in a minute after these messages."

The crowded detective muster room, its wall plastered with material devoted to catching the murderer, hummed with chatter. The videotape machine was switched off.

The front pages of the afternoon newspapers had banner headlines telling of the television scoop. This applied even more pressure to the growing homicide squad.

After a brief counter lunch at the pub, Gary and Lisa hurried across the floor of the large open-plan offices. Gary heard what he thought was his phone ringing. The moment he picked it up he knew it was Simpson. There was a slight pause before he spoke. Gary pushed the "hands-free" button on his phone so he could put the caller's voice on speaker.

"Hello, Leslie here."

"Peter Simpson here, mate. Is that the Abo cop who is looking for me?"

"Yes, I'm Aboriginal, Simpson. Where are you?" Gary spoke loudly. Lisa and Gary began gesturing in an insane manner to each other. Then she picked up a nearby phone in an attempt to trace the source of the call.

Simpson breathed heavily into the mouthpiece. "As you already know, I'm not that stupid."

"Okay, okay, what do you want?"

"I want to give myself up."

Gary felt his heart pumping. Word had spread quickly; the roomful of detectives swarmed the corner near the toilets in an attempt to hear.

"Tell me where and when, Peter. It's all up to you, mate. You're in control."

"Fucking right I'm in control!" he said angrily.

"Take it easy. Just tell me when and where, okay."

"Not yet mate. You'll know, but not fucking yet!"
The line went dead.

Gary slammed the phone down. "Jesus help me!" he cried out as he pushed the phone to the floor, his frustration transmitted to everyone within earshot.

Through the rain, a small red Toyota, it's headlights glaring into the darkness, pulled to a stop outside Evelyn's small row home. She got out of the car with two friends, laughing. Rehearsals had gone like a charm; the new performance was really shaping up. First she unlocked the three dead bolts then, standing in the hallway, she disarmed the alarm. Evelyn smelled the dampness as she entered the darkened house; quickly she switched the hallway light on.

"We'll go and get some wine and munchies to celebrate," the taller female said. "Do you need anything else?"

"No, I'm fine. I'll pack a few things and be ready when you get back," said Evelyn moving towards her bedroom.

As she packed Evelyn heard a constant dripping in the kitchen. She changed into some stretch tights and pulled on a sweater then headed for the kitchen. She planned to cook pasta and chicken in a tomato sauce tonight. She always kept a close watch on her diet but she needed her calories, she was a dancer, she burned them off.

When she switched the light on in the kitchen she saw the water leaking from the ceiling. A pool had formed on the plasterboard above the kitchen and seeped through.

"Oh no," she said. "Not the roof. More money!"

She went to the bathroom to fetch towels and placed them over the puddle. Then equipped with dining chair, flashlight and broom she went to the manhole in the hallway. On her toes she managed to probe open the access panel in the ceiling, which led to the roof. Waving the flashlight in the general direction above the kitchen she could see a hole had been cut in the metal roofing, it was large enough for a person to get through. The hairs on the back of her neck tingled, the adrenaline rushed to her brain; her eyes widened, forced forward from the pressure within.

Lisa finished eating a simple evening meal of omelette and toast. Cleaning the kitchen she broke into song. "It was never my intention . . . no, never my intention to . . . fall in love with you." She stretched to sweep the floor around the plastic garbage bin. The urgent sound of the telephone ringing interrupted her singing. Still bent over, Lisa was seized firmly from behind. She froze from fear.

"Hello Lisa," Peter said through clenched teeth. "See this, this is a fucking gun." He pushed the twenty-two-caliber revolver hard into her neck below her jaw. He had a hand clamped firmly over her mouth. "If you scream when I take my hand away I'll blow your fucking head off." Then he let it loose.

"Don't hurt me," Lisa said drawing breath through her nose.

"I'm not going to hurt you, Lisa, you are my prize."

The telephone continued to ring.

They swayed as if completing a crazy dance step as Peter's strength took control. He stepped back when he was certain she had calmed. He pulled her hair jerking her head back. Waving the gun wildly he said, "Where's the bedroom?" Not expecting an answer, he pushed her ahead of him down the hallway, still holding her firmly by the hair.

"How did you get in here?" she asked, trying to engage him in conversation.

"They can't put locks on everything, Lisa."

The telephone stopped ringing.

"You can have whatever you want, but please don't hurt me."

"I'll do what I fucking-well like," he said.

Lisa had learned that most attempts to reason with psychopaths failed but she had to try. He pushed her on the bed then hit her across the cheek with the barrel of the gun. Her skin lay open below her right eye, blood streamed down her face.

"Don't hurt me, don't hurt me," was all she could say. She was now in shock.

The telephone started again.

"Take your clothes off," he said as he sat at the foot of the bed. She scrambled quickly to her feet and did as he asked, shaking, fumbling, crying. "Not so fast," he said. "Slower. Much slower."

When she was naked he stood next to her, rubbing the tip of the gun around and over her nipples, smiling.

"Beautiful," he said. "Now get down on your knees." He unzipped his bulging trouser front.

The telephone stopped.

In her mind Lisa forced an image of Gary where she had just left him at the office. Help, I'm in trouble! Trouble! Trouble! Trouble! . . . was the message she sent out over and over.

"Suck me!" he said, spraying spittle through his teeth.

Lisa felt tears rolling down her cheeks as he pulled her head to him, forcing his penis onto her tightly closed lips. He placed the gun behind her ear, then pushing with a great deal of force, he barked his orders again. "Suck me! I love being sucked before fucking. Open up!"

Reluctantly, Lisa opened her mouth. He forced his bulging penis in. Then he began to move his pelvis, thrusting at her as he forced her head to him. She pulled away, just far enough to look up at him. He had his eyes tightly closed, contorting his face. He let out a moan with each thrust. Roughly, he pulled her head to him.

Suddenly, Lisa bit down. Desperately, she grabbed for the hand, which held the gun and pushed the barrel away from her. She climbed to one knee; clenching her right fist she swung with all her might and punched him flush on his testicles. Quickly she pulled back and punched again. A loud grunt came from her as she connected again. Simpson's mouth fell open, he was shocked and in pain. With all her strength, Lisa held the gun so it pointed at the ceiling. She felt his fingers squeeze the trigger, then the explosion. The heat from the blast blew onto her hand. Her knuckles turned white from the immense pressure she was applying. She pulled her right fist back and punched again. He still had her by the hair, she could feel some of it come away from her scalp as he tightened his grip. She punched again and again. She was losing her strength. She felt him pull on the trigger again; the gun exploded. She punched more desperately, knowing she could not hit hard any longer so she hit out as many times as she could.

Finally he let the gun fall from his hands. Lisa grabbed it, pushed it into his side and pulled on the trigger. It exploded twice then would only click. She continued to pull desperately on the trigger. Finally, she threw it away. Blood flowed from the area of Simpson's ribs but he still pulled at her hair as he screamed in agony. Lisa punched at his groin area again as Gary burst into the room, his gun firmly fixed at Simpson's head.

"Police!" he shouted. "Let her go!"

Simpson released his grip on Lisa. Loudly sobbing now she pulled back and punched him in the testicles again and again. Gary breathed deeply as he watched, allowing her her vengeance. Lisa fell to the floor exhausted. Gary pressed one foot heavily onto Simpson's head. "You're . . . under . . . arrest!" he said emphatically.

In the confusion Evelyn had come in and was at Lisa's side with a sheet. She pulled it over her as she cried, strived urgently for air. Blood had splashed and spilled about the small room.

Twenty minutes had passed, it seemed like hours to Lisa who was now dressed, sitting in her kitchen with Evelyn and Gary.

"When I found he had broken into my place through the roof, I panicked; I immediately went to phone you. Then I couldn't find your note with your number and address on it, I'd pinned it to my corkboard beside the phone. It was then that I knew that he had taken it. I was scared, I just phoned Emergency," Evelyn said, explaining slowly for Lisa to understand.

"They put the call straight through to me," Gary continued. "I was still in the office. When Evelyn told me your address was missing I knew. I came as fast as I could," he said, knowing it was not soon enough for Lisa's liking.

"I know you did. Thank you."

"We're taking him out now," a uniformed ambulance officer said as he and another supported Simpson to his feet.

"You go with him, he's your arrest," Lisa murmured softly.

Gary was adamant, "No, Lisa this is definitely your bust. He's yours."

Outside Lisa's small apartment building, nine police cars, all flashing red and blue lights, were strewn about as if placed there randomly by a strong wind. An ambulance sat askew across the footpath. Numerous reporters and television camera crews forged forward as Lisa came through the wide double doors, bright lights flared and camera units flashed. Pushing past them with Simpson firmly apprehended in handcuffs she stole a long look over her shoulder at Gary. They both smiled.

Five months later the birth of the newest Leslie was blissful. It was as easy as any such moment can be for a woman, Helen said. They named the boy James. Helen had been home from the hospital for one week when she and Gary received a postcard from Lisa. It had a photograph of night alpine skiers on Grouse Mountain near Vancouver and read:

Europe was very exciting; I really like being the foreigner. But Canada is something else. I skied until ten o'clock last night on Grouse Mountain. It was outstanding. I'd like to come back here, to stay for a while.

See you soon, Love and Mushy Stuff, Lisa. XXX

Epilogue

DAVID GUNDY

The details surrounding Mr. Gundy's real life struggle and violent death touched and outraged Aboriginals and non-Aboriginals alike: In 1957 at Casino, a town on the New South Wales north coast, a boy was born to Italian-Aboriginal parents. The boy's name would become known right across Australia. David Gundy never knew his Italian father but he did know he was descended from the Bungulung tribe whose homelands are the Lismore area. At the age of four he was taken away from his mother by Aboriginal "welfare" officials under the government's assimilation policy, which targeted part-Aboriginal children and was performed heartlessly. The idea was that the children were removed from their communities and were forced to behave like Englishmen. Rigidly enforced codes of conduct included that they not carry on their language and culture. This Orwellian behavioral modification practice ceased only in 1969.

David was first placed in a hostel. And was later given to Mr. and Mrs. Long, a white couple from Wyee. He had distinctly Italian features and grew up in white society but he always clung to his Aboriginality. David went to school at Wyee and Foster, finishing at grade ten. With the help of his foster father he excelled at carpentry. He had a few minor brushes with police: twice for dishonesty as a juvenile and two convictions for dishonesty as an adult.

After he left school, David lived in Newcastle where he worked in a mill. Later he moved to Sydney where he finally met the brothers and sisters he had never known. Through his newly found family he met Dolly Eatts, the love of his life. Dolly, from the Kalkdoon tribe, whose homelands take in the mining town of Mount Isa in Queensland, was instantly attracted to David.

David and Dolly began living together as husband and wife at Ashfield in 1976. Later they moved around. A good worker, David took on various jobs. He was a railway porter in Winton, Queensland, a miner in Mount Isa, a spray painter in Brisbane. In Sydney he became a storeman for an importer and then a forklift driver for a welding company. After a very rough start in life, David had "come good" by white man's standards.

In 1979, David and Dolly were asked by a relative of

Dolly to adopt her boy, Bradley, his white father had just committed suicide. Without hesitation the young couple took him in and treated him as their own.

On 24 April 1989, a sunny autumn day, at about 11:30 A.M. three young constables of the anti-theft squad stopped near an intersection behind Saint Mary's Cathedral to question a dark-skinned man who appeared to be breaking into a car. The man quickly pulled a gun and blasted away at the unsuspecting police, wounding two of them, Constable Donnelly and Constable McQueen. The man then made good his escape. Constable McQueen died from his wounds a few days later, pre-empting one of the largest man-hunts in New South Wales police history.

A police informant told police she thought the man they were looking for was a Pacific Islander, John Porter. She supplied police with six addresses where she had known Porter to stay; one of those addresses was the Marrickville home of Dolly Eatts and David Gundy. Dolly had known Porter when they were children and had only recently met up with him at a social gathering.

Search warrants were obtained for all six addresses.

In the early hours of 27 April, a command post was set up in an operations room at inner-city police offices in College Street. The police Air Wing and

Ambulance Services were alerted. An ambulance officer asked police for an indication of the sort of injuries that might be expected. He was told "gunshot wounds".

Sergeant Jim Brazel, a weapons instructor, assembled his team from the Special Weapons Operation Section (SWOS) outside the Gundy home in Marrickville. His officers were dressed in black, carried revolvers, shotguns with special flashlights attached and a sledgehammer. At 5.52 A.M. on 27 April 1989, they moved on the house.

After bashing their way inside the house the officers took houseguest Richard MacDonald into custody, he was sleeping in the lounge room immediately inside the door. Police also took another man, Mark Valentine, as well as David and Dolly's adopted son, Bradley. They had been asleep in the first bedroom off the hallway.

Sergeant Terry Dawson kicked in the door of the second bedroom; the events that followed have never been adequately clarified. A Royal Commission concluded that a brief struggle took place, with Mr. Gundy "probably approaching Sergeant Dawson in an attempt to take the shotgun away from him." David Gundy was shot dead with one blast at point blank range. The raid and killing took place in less than two minutes.

The police raid relied on a warrant which

authorized a team to move in on Mr. Gundy's home after 6.00 A.M. An urgent police call for ambulance assistance to attend a shooting at the Gundy house was logged at 5.54 A.M.

Richard MacDonald, the Gundy houseguest, was Dolly's brother. Richard had recently broken up with his wife and in the process, lost his house. He knew Porter from when they had been detained in a juvenile institution in Brisbane and had sometimes shared his flat in the inner city with Porter.

Dolly had taken Richard's six-year-old daughter to stay with their aunt in Mount Isa. That was where she was at the time of the raid. The police called her there to ask where Porter was. She was told there had been an accident but not that David had been killed. When she learned on television that David had been killed by police in their own home, she collapsed.

Until his death, Dolly Eatts and David Gundy had lived happily together for thirteen years.

Ted Pickering, the State police minister, was quick to endorse the police action at carefully conducted media conferences. Stern-faced, he told the public that police were feeling "uptight."

Three years after the killing neither Dolly nor her son had received an apology from the policeman who killed David, the Police Commissioner or the State Police Minister.

Most Australians were deeply shocked by the manner of Gundy's death and understood, perfectly, the distress and outrage Dolly Eatts was feeling. Not long after the killing, a video was broadcast on national television showing a police staff party at which two giggling policemen had arrived with their faces blackened with make-up. One had a hang-man's noose around his neck. The blackened policemen had signs with the names of two recent dead Aboriginal men on their chests, one was David Gundy, and the other was Lloyd Boney. (Mr. Boney had recently died under suspicious circumstances while in police custody). This police behavior out-raged the public: the Australian Prime Minister publicly announced this mockery of Aboriginal deaths to be a disgrace.

Mr. Hal Wootten QC prepared a report about the Gundy killing for the Royal Commission into Aboriginal deaths in custody. He found the raid was unlawful and that Mr. Gundy was a law-abiding man. He expressed his appall at the way the Gundy family had been treated after the raid.

More than four years after David Gundy was shot to death in his home, Justice James in the Supreme Court sanctioned an out-of-court settlement of seven hundred thousand dollars as compensation from the New South Wales Government to Mr. Gundy's de facto wife Dolly and son Bradley. Justice James noted in his verdict that Bradley had changed his surname from Eatts to Gundy, a name the boy bears proudly.